Harrison Morris

Tales from ten Poets

Harrison Morris

Tales from ten Poets

ISBN/EAN: 9783337174477

Printed in Europe, USA, Canada, Australia, Japan

Cover: Foto ©Andreas Hilbeck / pixelio.de

More available books at **www.hansebooks.com**

ROBERT BROWNING

TALES FROM TEN POETS. BY HARRISON S. MORRIS

IN THREE BOOKS
THE FIRST BOOK

WITH PORTRAITS

PHILADELPHIA
J. B. LIPPINCOTT COMPANY
1893

PRINTED BY J. B. LIPPINCOTT COMPANY, PHILADELPHIA.

A WORD TO THE READER.

THERE is a deep-grained love in humanity for a story pure and simple. The fireside gossip who dishes up the sweet morsels of the past, has little art at his command. He can give nothing save the bare skeleton of a tradition, a tragedy, or a bit of drollery. His are the broadest and ruggedest of touches, and he has gained his end and pleased his audience if he has only sketched, in boldest outline, facts whose interest lies solely in themselves and their relative arrangement.

Art, however, is quite another and a nobler thing. The simple facts which jut up from human intercourse like rough boulders, become, after a while, covered and softened with the foliage and minute mosses of art. The prosaic outlines pass away into something no less true, but lovelier and finer. The rock beneath gives endurance. The grass above brings appealing beauty, and this renders the endurance forever precious.

In the pages to come, the reader who loves

a story for its own sake may find, if he pleases, the enduring rock stripped of its verdurous robe, the story laid bare of its artistic medium and made to stand by itself. He may see what durable foundations lie beneath the great achievements of poetic art which belong to our own century and our own tongue; and he will, moreover,—for the thing is assured to the man or woman of taste who enters even in so rudimentary a manner upon the perusal of these noble masterpieces,—he will perforce find himself led by their indestructible charm into an elevating desire to know the poems themselves.

In needless apology for re-immortalizing the old story of Endymion, Keats wrote, "I hope I have not at too late a day touched the beautiful mythology of Greece and dulled its brightness." I, likewise, but in needed apology, hope that I have not dulled the brightness of these beautiful creations of the age of Victoria by rendering them into unsympathetic prose. To one who cares for them and holds them dear as among the most lasting and subtile products of our contemporary life, it is an irreverent act to sever them from their natural settings. Yet Mr. Andrew Lang finds it in his heart to justify the act. "So determined are we not to read tales in verse," says he, "that prose renderings, even of the epics, nay, even of the Attic dramas, have come more or less into vogue."

With this genial endorsement, then, and with the hope that these prose versions may lead every reader who is not already acquainted with them to a knowledge of the famous originals, I submit them to an age which has been called scientific because it too often disregards what is beautiful simply for being so.

I have tried to adhere to the central idea, and even the detail, of each poem, as strictly as was consistent with the production of a well-rounded and complete tale in prose. Entertainment and diversion must be the chief aim in such a collection as this, and where the more complex effects allowed to a poem have hindered the development of the prose story, I have, but with a reverent touch, endeavored to disengage the story and let it tell itself straight on to the climax.

Much is lost by such a process to those who love poetry; but to those who care for the reason without the rhyme there is—should the teller have done justice to the tale—infinite store of delight still left.

H. S. M.

CONTENTS OF BOOK I.

LIST OF ILLUSTRATIONS.

BOOK I.

THE RING AND THE BOOK.

ROBERT BROWNING.

THE RING AND THE BOOK.

I.

THE Comparini, man and wife, Pietro and Violante, were yesterday as happy as any prosperous couple in Rome. To-day they lie dead in the church of San Lorenzo in Lucina.

Crowds from the populous Corso have streamed into the aisles all day long to have a look at the murdered pair, where they rest on either side of the altar. There is an endless buzz of question and counter-question, of curiosity and sympathy, and of hot vengeance uttered against Count Guido Franceschini, who is known to have done the deed.

It is a motley throng inside the old church. Here the scarlet robe of a cardinal moves down the midst of dark-cloaked idlers from the streets; over there, in faded homespun, lounges some peasant come into town for the holiday. They push on to the chancel, throw up their eyes, cross themselves, look hastily at the dead and the notched triangular dagger lying at their

13

feet, and then give place to the pressing lines behind. All the world knew the old pair, and all the world has come to talk the tragedy over. Once within, they find it hard to leave. They have climbed the columns, and perched themselves on the chapel-rail, jumped over and broken the painted wood-work, crammed the organ-loft, and literally packed every corner of the sacred place.

"Not in seventy years," says toothless Luca Cini, bending on his staff,—"not in all the seventy years I have seen bodies set forth has there been a day like it."

Now this is the story of those two, lying there with faces stabbed out of recognition by an enemy who thus vindicated his honor, according to the wont of the noblemen of his day.

It was the year of our Lord 1679, and Rome was the religious centre of the world. Pope Innocent the Twelfth sat upon the papal throne, a feeble old man who ruled benignly but firmly the great realm, both spiritual and temporal, which belonged to the church. In his service were numberless prelates high and low, and a throng of nuns and monks and friars, who carried the ecclesiastical power into every rank of society. They were the judges in the city courts, the officers of the municipal govern-

ment, the scholars who preserved and taught
the older learning, and they led, moreover, the
social world of Rome, whether it dwelt in the
palaces of the Corso or lived a simpler life in
the Via Vittoria.

And in the Via Vittoria, plain, substantial, the
abode of good citizens who had wealth enough
to bring them leisure, even if too little to in-
dulge in many luxuries,—in this pleasant thor-
oughfare lived Pietro and Violante Comparini.
They had been born in that quarter of the city
seventy-odd years before, and remained there
throughout their lives. They, like all the rest
around them, married young, but they were
childless, and this was a disappointment to
Pietro and a distress to his good wife, for
Pietro's wealth, such as it was, belonged to him
only during his life, and would pass into the
hands of some distant heir when he should die.
Yet they had led a careless and happy existence
in their city house and in the villa out in the
Pauline district just beyond the walls. This
rural place Pietro had bought to retire to for
little frolics such as men in his condition loved
to plan with congenial friends who had a tooth
for good wine and loved free laughter. But with
its dark sides hidden in foliage and thick trees
overhanging its roof, the villa was after all just
the place to put murder into an enemy's head.

Such idle living is, however, a costly thing even if one have an ample income to draw upon, and the funds of the Comparini were not by any means inexhaustible. As the years went by they began to feel the drain upon their resources, and before very long they actually found themselves in debt. So, like most people who have gained a distinction for liberality among neighbors and friends, they clung blindly to the reputation, and continued to load their board for flattering guests even while they held out their hands for the papal bounty, which in that day was dispensed to the needy who were too respectable to beg.

But the sole way out of the dilemma was to secure an heir. Pietro's income was exhausted, that was plain enough. The original wealth whence it was drawn, however, remained in the custody of the law, and should the miracle ever occur that he and Violante might still have born to them an heir, then the coveted money would fall into their hands and all would be well. So Pietro prayed earnestly for an heir to his fallen house, but Violante, more practical though less nice in honor, went secretly to work to fulfil the pious yearning of her husband.

There was a place in Rome down past San Lorenzo, beyond labyrinths of ancient dwellings, where, at the end of a certain black and dingy court, stood a house which Violante one day sought and entered. She had left the Via Vittoria book in hand as if to hear mass, as was her daily wont, in San Lorenzo church; but book and pious face were assumed to deceive Pietro, who must not know of her secret errand into the dark places of the city. There was a light at the top of the house, and she mounted by the filthy steps, holding tight to the cord which did service for baluster, until she had reached the last landing. She groped towards the half-open door where the dim light fell through, and entered on her hidden quest. A half-clad woman started up at her footsteps.

"What, you back already!" she cried. "Have mercy on me, poor sinner that I am!" But seeing only a woman, her voice changed from terror to entreaty, and "What may your pleasure be?" she civilly asked of the undaunted Violante.

Now, Violante had long kept in mind the object of her present visit, and she had noticed this woman over her open-air washing at the cistern by Citorio, noticed and envied her shapely figure, and had tracked her home to her forlorn house-top, whither she had now come to tempt her by proposing an unlawful bargain. The talk was short between them, for the wretched washerwoman was only too willing to earn an addition to her scanty wages,

and Violante was disinclined to linger long in
such compromising intercourse. They parted
at the stairway, and as Violante descended into
the darkness below the woman repeated, in a
loud whisper above her on the landing, the
terms of the agreement,—

"Six months hence, then, a person whom you
trust is to come and fetch the babe away, no
matter what its sex. The price is to be kept
secret, and the child to be yours."

Violante was triumphant. Here was the
whole trouble solved by a single deft stroke of
diplomacy. To be sure, it was an unworthy sub-
terfuge and weighed a trifle on her conscience,
but the heirs to Pietro's wealth must look out
for themselves, and as for the stain of such a
compact as she had just made, that must be
atoned for by redoubled fervor in devotion;
and, so thinking, she hurried off to church, gain-
ing her place just in time for the Magnificat,
which she uttered with unusual energy.

When she arrived at home Violante revealed
to Pietro a startling and joyous piece of news.
Her constant orisons, she said, and charitable
work had brought her a fulfilment of her great
longing. She must keep in-doors for the next
half-year, and then, maybe,—and she coupled
the news with an elderly caress,—maybe they
might at last be blessed with an heir to restore

their fortunes and brighten their fast-approaching age.

So one day Pietro found himself the father of a little black-eyed girl, and with the conscious pride of mature paternity, as well as the inward satisfaction that now his financial troubles were likely to be mended, at least for a time, he and his wife bore the infant to San Lorenzo church, where the Curate Ottoboni christened it, with the prodigality of names then in vogue, Francesca Vittoria Pompilia Comparini.

Violante played her part well, and no shadow of suspicion crossed the mind of her husband or of the gossips of the Via Vittoria. Whether or not the dangerous secret preyed upon her mind, she bore herself as a mother should, and did with unfaltering assurance what was needful in the ceremony of baptism. Hers was a calculating mind, and she had carefully planned and now as carefully executed a hazardous scheme, which, she reflected, had for its end a justifying benefit both for her husband and herself. Moreover, was it not a worthy act to rescue from squalid surroundings and degrading influences a child that might prove a delight to their barren age and grow to useful and perhaps beautiful womanhood? Such thoughts ran through her mind as she stood beside her husband at the font, and with them her common-

place nature postponed for a time the inevitable
reassertion of conscience.

But Pietro in all the luxury of his new father-
hood was a vain and delighted man. He bore
the little Pompilia home with a thousand ca-
resses, and from that day forth he was her play-
mate and her slave. He romped with her on
the floor, taught her, as she grew, many a childish game, and year by year measured her in-
creasing height against the walls of the shaded
villa beyond the gates.

Poverty, however, had always of late lurked
at Pietro's heels, and one day, with scarce a
warning, he found himself in absolute need.
He had squandered his inherited income, had
idled away his opportunities to repair it, and
now in his old age he was destitute and helpless. But Violante was a wife of many resources, and her busy mind went to work with
all its old vigor to solve the new difficulty. They
still had one possession which might retrieve
their fortunes. Pompilia was now a grown girl,
with great dark eyes and a bounty of black
hair. She had, moreover, the sweet touch of that
first youth which is a potent charm to most
men, but which appeals with a peculiar zest to
the jaded taste of a man of the world. She
was over-young, to be sure, for marriage, but in
the Italy of that day a young girl stepped out

of childhood directly into wedlock, and immaturity of mind and of character was overlooked by wooers who sought only beauty or wealth.

It was the crafty Violante's plan, then, to carry her attractive goods to the most favorable market. She had grown attached to the child, because of its loving traits and infantile charm, and because it had so well served her purpose, but the family need weighed heavily on her now, and, like many another ambitious dame with only half her motives, she set deliberately to work to secure at one stroke for Pompilia a wealthy husband and for herself and Pietro a snug fireside protective against want, with even a little luxury thrown in if that were possible.

Now, the desperate state of Pietro's affairs was unknown as yet to his neighbors, and he had managed thus far with the remnants of his credit to eke out a respectable appearance. No whisper of the inward anxiety was allowed to mar the customary outward thrift, and the old reputation for fortune and prosperity was untouched by rumor. This being the case, Pompilia, with fresh young beauty and the repute of considerable wealth, was an eligible match likely to be snapped at by a suitor whose own fortunes while not exhausted still needed replenishing, or by some elderly seeker after a youthful spouse.

Pompilia **herself was** just thirteen years old, and knew nothing of the trials which beset her parents. **She had lived a** careless and happy life in the garden of the **villa, and scarcely ever,** save when she went to San Lorenzo church, saw the great world outside its walls. **She** had a sole friend in the early times, **Tisbe, a** neighbor's child, **whom** Violante brought in **to play with** her **on** rainy afternoons; and **the two would** trace each other's **fortunes** in the woven **stories of the household tapestry.**

"**Tisbe, that's you, there,** with a half-moon **on** your hair-knot and **a** spear in your hand,—a **huntress.** See, you are following the stag, and **a** great blue scarf blows out at your back."

"And there you are, Pompilia, with green leaves growing from your finger-ends and all the **rest of you** turned into a sort of tree."

Then they would laugh together and play out **the** tales pictured for them through the folds of **the dim** old hangings; or they would often run **off to the** vineyard and sit in the shade of **the** vine-leaves for whole mornings together.

Such childish happiness had wrought in little **Pompilia** a thoughtful and sympathetic nature, **but she had** grown up without mental training and unconscious of the simplest experiences of life. She **could** neither read nor write; she had **scarcely known one of the opposite sex save**

the fatherly old Pietro, and she was entirely
ignorant that such a thing as giving in marriage existed.

But one day as Pietro was taking an after-
dinner doze and Pompilia, in some far-away
chamber, was busy at her broider-frame, there
came a priest to the Via Vittoria: a smooth-
mannered and sleek-faced personage in the
habit of an Abate, who asked for Violante with
a conscious air of knowing that she was within
and alone.

" Might he speak ?"

" Yes," came promptly from in-doors, with a
flutter of skirts, and he entered and seated himself with the suave grace of one used to more
elevated interviews. He begged leave to present
himself as the Abate Paolo, the younger brother
of a Tuscan house, whose actual representative
was the Count Guido Franceschini; and then,
glossing his great flap hat with the palm of his
hand or reaching down to smooth the wrinkles
from his shapely stocking, but always keeping
a keen gray eye fixed on the flattered dame, he
descanted on the house of the Franceschini,
how old they were, what ancestors they boasted
of, and a score of other notable things fit to
turn the head of a much wiser mother than
the susceptible Violante.

" But we are not rich," he said, with an ap-

parent burst of candor,—"that is, not so poor
either.   One can't have everything, you know.
We are well enough off to support the reputation of the house, and then we are in the way
to fortune,"—and he leaned forward with a con-
fidential lowering of the voice, as if to speak
into Violante's ravished ear,—"and to fortune
better than the best.   Well, my good madam,
you see, if we could but keep Count Guido
patient for a little while, constant to his own
interests and friendly with the Cardinal whom
he serves, we should one day wear—it is promised us—the red cloth that keeps a whole household warm.   But he is restless, dissatisfied, and,
moreover, he's slipping on into years, and years
make men want certainties,—not promises alone,
not promises."   And the Abate emphasizing the
word, Violante also said, seriously,—

"Quite right, quite right, your Reverence;
promises make poor living."

"What I was about to say," continued the
Abate. "Promises make poor living indeed; and,
in truth, my brother Guido is home-sick,—longs
for the old sights and usual faces again; he has,
poor fellow, no ecclesiastical tastes; he's a cold
nature, humble but self-sustaining. Ah, poor
brother Guido! he cares little enough for the
pomp of Rome. Dear me! he'd rather live in
his dingy palace, as vast almost as a quarry and

nearly as bare, or up at his villa on the hill-side by Vittiano."

Violante interjected here a pleased " Indeed !" to signify her sense of the honor done her by such explicit revelations of family affairs, and then the Abate went on :

" Yes, he talks of nothing else ; it's the palace and the villa, the villa and the palace, all day long,—enough to make one's ears ache. And lately nothing will do but he must fly away from Rome post-haste to cheer his mother's old age by domesticating with her in the palace ; and a new idea has struck him too. He must not go back alone ; he must carry a wife with him to enliven his mother's declining years and inspire her with hope and gayety,—so he says."

Violante was hardly able to suppress her desire to offer Pompilia then and there, and to sing her praises as a wife, but she had a glimmering sense that a slight resistance would be seemly, and she merely betrayed the wish by a sharp little movement forward in her chair and a lifting of her hands from her lap.

" La, now," she said, " and a very good thing for him to do."

" True, true," continued the Abate, " a very rational thing to do," and he smiled gayly at the pleased old dame. " Ought now a man to interpose if his brother contemplates so wise a step? There's no making Guido great; that's out of the question. Why, then, not let him for once be happy? But he must be protected from designing matrons who covet the distinction of such an alliance without being able to give sufficient in return. Yes, Guido needs the watchful interest of his brothers,"—the Abate here cast down his eyes in humble deprecation of his own merits: "he must not be allowed to make a *mésalliance*. That at least we must forestall."

"Little danger," said the discreet Violante, "with so experienced a hand to guide him." The Abate made a profound bow and proceeded:

"No, signora, we are not anxious for name and fame; we have sufficient of them already. But if some pure and charming woman, untainted by the world, and all tenderness and truth, could be found,—some girl, not too wealthy, to match with Guido's own moderate fortune,— but, of course, with a sufficient dowry,—if such a girl could be discovered, she would indeed be the ideal wife for Count Guido."

Violante said nothing, but she showed by conscious interest that she had taken the bait so craftily suggested by the Abate, and was ready when he had twitched the line to be handsomely landed.

"And now," he began, with an assumption of
ignorance and an insinuating voice, "is it not
true that you, Signora Violante, keep hidden
here in this very house a lily of a daughter
such as we seek for Count Guido? Ah, I have
guessed your secret!" he laughed, with mock-
threatening finger raised. "You conceal here
under your sheltering mother-wing a wife
worthy of Guido's house and heart."

"By no means, your Reverence," said Violante, with becoming humility; "merely my
little daughter Pompilia, unworthy, believe me,
such an honor."

"Ah," said the gallant Abate, "you cannot
long hide such a beauty from the light. But I
merely came to see. I have spoken frankly
and openly. I could do no less." Here he
patted his well-shaped calf again, and then,
straightening up with a shrug, said, "If any
harm's done—well, the matter's at least off my
mind, and I humbly ask your pardon, signora,
for the intrusion."

He rose now with a clerical dignity abandoned
during their conversation and grandly kissed
the devout Violante's hand. Then he bowed
low and left her.

When he was quite gone, Violante rubbed her
eyes awhile in sheer bedazzlement, and then ran
off to waken Pietro and tell him the wonderful

news. Her more practical husband rubbed his
eyes in turn, looked very knowing, and indeed
not a little puzzled too, took up his cane and
hat, and then sallied forth to the Square of
Spain, towards the Boat-fountain, where his
gossips were wont to lounge and exchange the
news. He made some display of his latest
honor, and expected to be congratulated on
such good fortune, but he only got well laughed
at for his pains. They told him with blunt
jocosity just who his visitor was: the brother
of Count Guido Franceschini, whose paternal
acres were a stubble-field and brick-heap. There
used to be a palace, but it was long ago
burned down. To be sure, he was a count,
but he hadn't a coin in his pouch,—nothing
left to support a noble name but sloth, pride,
and rapacity. Wanted to go home, did he?
Well, let Pietro help him; he'd not get home
without assistance.

"As for this Abate Paolo," said an old gray-
beard who sat on the fountain-step, "he's a
shrewder mouse. He's done well here in Rome,—
fattened on the church and made a comfortable
nest. But Guido's had to shift for himself, and
now his Cardinal's cast him off, and his last
shift's this of yours. He's snuffed your snug
little annuity, and in return would make your
girl a lady, forsooth! There," and he looked

with a derisive smile up at Pietro, " don't brag
to us. Do you suppose Count Guido 'd stoop to
you and yours if he had one coin to chink
against another? Bah!"

So Pietro went home again disenchanted and
rueful, yet glad that the matter had ended where
it did and no harm done.

The marriage being thus impossible, all else
followed in due course : Paolo serenely heard
his fate; Count Guido bore the blow with resig-
nation; and poor disappointed Violante wiped
away a tear or two, renouncing her golden
dreams with bitter reluctance. But she praised
through her tears Pietro's prompt sagacity and
affected to acquiesce in his wiser decree.

Thus all went well for a day or so ; then Violante, as she one night fondled Pompilia in her
arms, whispered to her,—

" And what if a gay cavalier should come to-
morrow to see my little Pompilia?" And she
held the girl off and looked smilingly into her
great dark eyes. " And if he does come, Pompilia must let him take her hand and kiss it;
and then some fine night we shall all go off to
San Lorenzo church, and you and he will be
married at the altar; and after that we will
come home again and leave the cavalier, and—
that's all. But, you naughty girl, you must say
nothing about it,—not even to papa Pietro,—

now, do you hear? Girl-brides must not tell
secrets. And won't it be a gay lark to steal away
and never let him know ?"

So on the morrow Count Guido came and
paid his devoirs to his intended bride. He was
in pitiable contrast with the young and beautiful girl he was to marry. Hook-nosed and yellow, with a great bush of a beard, he looked like
an ancient owl clad in the garb of a Roman
nobleman. But Pompilia was ignorant of the
commonest usages of life, and wedlock for her,
even with such a groom, had none of the ter-
rors which it would have had for a more mature
and experienced woman.

The next night, through a driving December
storm, the girl and her mother, well cloaked
and veiled, set out for San Lorenzo, and there
met the Abate Paolo at the altar-side. Two
tapers shivered in the damp chill of the church,
and Pompilia, standing in mute expectancy,
heard the outer doors locked behind her, as if
barring out help and hope.

"Quick, lose no time!" cried the priest, and
straightway down from behind the altar, where
he was in hiding, stepped Count Guido, who
caught Pompilia's hand. The Abate then went
hurriedly through the service, and at last pro-
nounced them man and wife. Then the two
brothers drew aside and talked together, while

Pompilia, trembling and dismayed, crept down and joined her mother, who was weeping. They were noticed no further, and stole on tiptoe to the door, which was now unlocked. It had stopped raining, and they hastened through the dark wet streets for home. At the house-door Violante turned, and, placing a finger across Pompilia's lips, whispered,—

"Not a word to papa Pietro. Girl-brides never breathe a word. You hear?"

Cheerily Pietro welcomed them home with not a little banter.

"What do these priests mean," he said, "by praying folks to death in such weather as this? Christmas at hand, too, to wash off our sins without need of rain."

Violante gave Pompilia's hand a timely squeeze, and the young bride kissed the old man and said not a word.

II.

THREE weeks of Pompilia's life had uneventfully passed, when one morning as she sat singing alone in her chamber at her embroidery-frame two or three loud voices, with now and then a sob and the names " Guido," " Paolo," angrily spoken, broke the silence and startled her to her feet. She ran into the room where the voices came from, to see what was the mat-

ter, and there stood the Count and his brother
the Abate with his sly face nowise dismayed,
while Pietro seemed all red and angry, scarce
able to stutter out his wrath. Violante stood
by sobbing as he reproached her,—

" You have murdered us,—me and yourself
and the poor child !"

" Murdered or not, Signor Pietro Comparini,"
Guido interposed, " your child is now my wife.
I claim her, and have come to take her."

But Paolo, with more dexterity, put suavely
in : " Consider, Signor Pietro—or—kinsman, if
I may call you so, what is the good of all your
sagacity except to give you wisdom in such a
strait as this ? The two are irrevocably man
and wife ; that I guarantee, whether it please
you or not. Now, we look to you for counsel,
not violence, since the thing cannot be undone.
Tell us what to do and we will gladly follow
your advice," and Paolo smiled craftily, sensible
that the game was wholly in his own hands ;
the while Violante, sobbing all the faster, murmured, " Yes, all, all murdered. Oh, my sin,
my secret !" and other such contrite fragments,
consolatory to no one in particular.

Then Pompilia began to surmise the truth.
Something false and underhand had happened,
for which Violante was to blame and she to be
pitied, for they all spoke of her, though none

addressed her. She stood there mute until Pietro embraced her and said,—

"Withdraw, my child!" then turning to the rest, "She is not likely at this stage to be helpful to the sacrifice. Do you want the victim by while you estimate its value? For her sake I consent, then, to hear you talk; but she must retire. Go, child, and pray God to help the innocent!"

Pompilia went away then and knelt to pray; but soon Violante came in to her with swollen eyes and hushful movements of the mouth, to make believe matters were coming right again.

"You are too young," she sobbed, "and cannot understand yet. Your father did not understand at first. I wanted to benefit us all three, and when he failed to see my meaning, why, I tried to do it without his aid; but now he confesses he was wrong, and the trouble's half over. To be sure it was right to give you a husband with a noble name and a palace and no end of other pleasant things! What do you care about youth and good looks?—this is the kind of a man to keep the house and love his wife. We lose a daughter, to be sure, but we gain a son, that's all, and now Pietro begins to be reasonable."

Pompilia strove to pacify her agitated mother

I.—c

and made cheerful assent to all she asked, then
Violante went on:

"It's to be arranged, my dear child, so that
we shall never separate. Papa Pietro and I
are to go to Arezzo to live with you and the
Count, in a fine palace where you will be the
queen; and you'll forgive your unhappy old
mother, now, won't you,—there's a sweet?"

"Forgive her! what for?" exclaimed Pompilia.
"Everything is right, mother, if only you will
stop crying. There, there, you have done no
harm, and it was all for the best after all!"

Then Violante kissed her fervently and took
her back to where her father leaned opposite
Count Guido, who stood eying him as a butcher
might eye a cast ox that accepts its fate and
ceases to struggle. Paolo looked archly on,
touching his brow with the pen-point now and
then to subdue a look of triumph, and when
Pompilia came up to them he said impressively,
with a dignified gesture towards her and the
Count,—

"Count Guido, take your lawful wife until
death do part you."

While Violante was absent with Pompilia
the terms of the marriage contract had been
agreed upon. Pietro was induced, partly by
coercion, partly by persuasion, but more than
all else by the inward consciousness of his own

ruined condition, to assign to his son-in-law, Count Guido, all his possessions of every kind whatever, in return for which the Count promised to support Pietro and his wife during the rest of their lives in his palace at Arezzo. The Roman household was to strike fresh roots into Tuscan soil. Pompilia was to pay her portion of the charge with her dowry, and the rest was to come out of the empty purse of Pietro.

There was a chuckle of satisfaction in Pietro's throat upon making terms so helpful to his broken fortunes at so opportune a moment, and the inward gratification he derived from this went far to heal the wound made by the disobedience of his wife and the risk it involved to his daughter's happiness. On their part, Paolo and Guido were equally gleeful over so favorable a settlement. Paolo's eyes twinkled with insuppressible exultation at having so far achieved his dearest hope of inveigling old Comparini into an agreement which should restore the noble house of Franceschini. They had, in short, each outwitted the other, and laid up an endless store of rancor for the bitter future that was approaching.

Thus, with only the twilight of their lives still to spend, Pietro and his spouse went to Arezzo, eager to enjoy the lord- and ladyship gained by their doubtful bargain. Guido, on his part,

longed for the tranquillity purchased by his new
venture, and looked with relief towards a future
free from display and ambitions. But the Comparini were anxious to begin where he had left
off. This was not a promising state in which to
enter upon such an arrangement as theirs; and
a woful want of harmony was apparent even
during the first week of their common residence
at the so-called palace.

"This," cried Pietro and Violante in a breath,
—"this the Count, the palace, the privilege and
luxury that were promised us! For this have
we exchanged our liberty, our competence, and
our darling child! Why, this is a sepulchre, a
mere stone-heap, a disgrace to the very street
it stands in, and that the vilest street in the
whole town as it is."

They harped in turn upon their wrongs. Now
it was Violante who mourned the loss of her
accustomed diet and inveighed against the mea-
greness of Guido's fare; then Pietro, with a plaint
for the Via Vittoria and the pleasant villa in
the Pauline.

"Where is the neighborliness and feasts and
holidays," ruefully asked Violante,—"ay, even
the cheerful sun that used to shine for us
in Rome? Where are they? We are robbed
and starved and frozen. We will have justice.
We will go to the courts." And because Count

Guido's mother, old Lady Beatrice, made an effort to placate the enraged dame, but was slow to abdicate her post of mistress, she was called a score of hard names, devil and dragon and what not, too severe for frail humanity to bear; but the elderly noblewoman stood upon her ancestral dignity and only infuriated her opponent the more with her provoking contempt.

All this Count Guido suffered with assumed forbearance, for he did not relish a rupture with the Comparini before he should be blessed with an heir as an additional pledge of his title to Pietro's fortune. But after four months' experience of such a life, with Pietro trumpeting his wrongs at church and in the market-place, and Violante pouring hers into any pair of ears that would listen,—after the exhaustion of all his calculating and wary patience the Count was glad at last to get rid of them, even at the risk of endangering his nicely-plotted scheme.

So, their worst done, saving the final breach, the Comparini one day renounced their share of the bargain; flung in Guido's face the debt due them for maintenance never rendered; left their heart's darling, as they said, at the mercy of her husband's cruelty; bade Arezzo to rot, and cursed it one and all; then travelled on vociferating and enraged to Rome.

Now, it was Jubilee week in Rome when Pietro

and Violante arrived there. The good old Pope Innocent the Twelfth had ordained a celebration of his eightieth birthday, and the city was given over to festivities. He had also benignly de-creed a pardon for minor offences of conscience, and a leniency towards baser crimes, provided the offender confessed and was shriven of his guilt during the week of Jubilee. This set the injured Violante to brooding over her long-hid-den sin against Pietro. She had never quite been able to clear her conscience of the stain of having entered into the unrighteous bargain for the purchase of Pompilia. No evil had, she tried to believe, ever arisen from it. Pietro was still alive, and the distant relatives who would have inherited his money were in no wise defrauded of their due. On the other hand, the child had been reclaimed, and much good had thus actually been accomplished. Never-theless the sense of guilt clung to her through the years, though she had tried to throw it off by making Pompilia happy, by marrying her into a noble family, and by sacrificing all she possessed for the girl's sake. Now, however, that she found herself in Rome with such bitter experiences rankling in her mind and a deep hatred of Guido inciting her to any extreme for the sake of revenge, now that she might so easily gain the good Pope's absolution, and at

the same time deal a deadly blow at Count
Guido, by imperilling his wife's dowry, she began to think more constantly of her sin and
more seriously and deeply to repent of it.

So she muffled and veiled herself and went
one day to church, where she entered with the
straggling throngs and made her way to the
confessional. There she knelt down, with beating heart, and in a hushed and broken voice revealed to the listening ear all the odious details
of her plot: how she had bought Pompilia,
palmed her off on the unsuspecting Pietro, and
then married her to Count Guido. The reply
came like a note from the trump of fate. Before she could be absolved of guilt she must
make restitution.

"Do your part," said the measured voice.
"Tell your husband's defrauded heirs. Tell
your husband himself, who has been entrapped
into paternal love for a child not his own. Tell
Count Guido, your son-in-law,—tell him, and
bear his just anger. Then, when you have duly
done penance, come hither, and you may be par-
doned; not before."

When Violante arose from her knees her mind
was firmly made up. She went directly home
and made a contrite avowal of her wrong-doing
to Pietro, who listened in astonishment, yet
with no visible emotion, to her startling revela-

tion. He was stunned by the news, but there was a mitigating note which sounded through it all and made it bearable. He loved Pompilia truly, and to have been told this about her six months ago would have wounded him like cold steel, but now all was different. If Pompilia were not their child, then the disastrous bargain with Count Guido was cancelled and the remnant of his means was still his own. Perhaps, too, he thought, with the leap at a hoped-for conclusion common to us all when the clouds of misfortune seem about to break, perhaps when the Count hears that he has married a base-born waif he will cast her off, and we shall then have our dear Pompilia back again as well as her dowry.

There was only one way in which Pietro might bring this new turn of affairs to Guido's notice, and that lay through the civil courts. The Comparini were now actually destitute, and had been obliged, since their return to Rome, to live upon the indulgence of old friends who were little enough inclined thus to pay for past hospitalities. Hence on the morrow Pietro began an action to recover his pledge from Count Guido, and Violante blushingly appeared and made public declaration of her fault. She renounced her motherhood, and prayed the law of Rome to interpose and redress the injury

which had resulted from her misdeed to her and
hers.

Guido, on his part, made answer that the
story was one long falsehood invented to rob
him of his own and gain a shameless revenge
for fancied wrongs. And thus, with crimina-
tion and recrimination, bitter reproach and fierce
reply, they fought out the cause before the ecclesiastical judges who tried, in those times, all
the cases within the jurisdiction of the Church.

At last the trial was finished and the court
gave its verdict. The wise judges inclined to
the moderate middle course. They held the
child to be a waif; but, lest Guido should suffer by such a decision, they adjudged him the
dowry even while they acknowledged it not to
belong to her. It was to be looked upon as a
partial repayment for the injury done him, not
his by right of marriage. As for Pietro's contract of renunciation of his own estate, that
was to be annulled, for he, at least, was no
party to the misdoing.

Such a decree was satisfactory neither to
Guido nor to Pietro, and each pleaded immediately for a reinvestigation of the case. This
proceeding necessarily caused delay, and the
matter therefore rested for the time in an un-
settled condition.

Hence the bitterness on all sides was deepened,

and Guido, whose sinister disposition had been intensified by disappointment and ridicule, began to vent upon his wife the rage he could not visit upon her parents. He was left alone in the grim ruin of a palace with his brooding hatred of Pietro and Violante, and the only subject with which to satisfy his longing for revenge was his innocent wife. Suppose he should cast her off, turn her out of doors? But the dowry was in the way. He must not part from her or repudiate her, or his right to the one thing for which he married her would come into question. No, he must not be foolish. But she could be made to suffer. There was nothing to hinder that. And suffer she should, if his pent-up malice could torture her or bring her into shame. Oh, how he hated her! Every accent of her childlike voice, every movement of her tender lips, made him think of the deep insult, the cruel wrong to his noble house inflicted by her plebeian kin.

He laid his plans with cool deliberation. If Pompilia could be induced in some way to fly from his house and follow her parents to Rome, if she should break forth in open revolt and voluntarily leave him, then there would be no question of his ownership in the dowry. He would be rid of her and confirmed in his possession of her money at one fortunate stroke. His would be the universal sympathy, hers the general reproach, and thus he might enjoy the dear boon of revenge upon the whole three at once. Everything was to gain by this method, and he went craftily to work upon it.

To Pompilia, the news that she was not the daughter of Pietro and Violante had come with little effect. Her love for them was undiminished, and she felt sure of their love for her. It was simply one of the phases of the endless wrangle with her husband, and she could not understand it any better than she understood all the rest of the puzzling and distressing quarrel. But one day as she sat alone, musing, perhaps, upon the old childish pleasures of her home, and longing to be with her parents again, Guido came in to her with a conciliatory look and bent over her, reaching a paper for her to see, on which were pencilled some faint lines of writing. "Look," he said, pointing to the text with a long finger, "I have written you a letter here to my brother the Abate. He will want to know how we get on together, the household news, and this and that. Mere compliment and courtesy. You cannot write, you say? But it would please Paolo to hear from you, and you can easily re-trace those pencil lines in ink. Sign it so," and he pointed to her name at the end, "and let me send it when you have finished.

It will be a kindly thing, a sisterly act, in truth,
and Paolo will be pleased."

He watched her and guided her pen sometimes as she wrote, and when she had reached
the end he took the letter from her and went
to his own apartment, chuckling to himself as
he read what she had been made to say. She
was rejoiced, so the letter ran, that her vile
kinsfolk at last were gone. She revealed, piece
by piece, all the depths of their malice, and how
they even laid an injunction on her before they
left that she should allure some young gallant
to her side, and plot with him to rob her husband, then burn the house down, taking care
previously to poison all the inmates overnight,
and, thus accompanied, fly to Rome and there
join fortunes with them once more.

With such a letter in hand the Abate did much
in Rome to prejudice his powerful friends against
the Comparini and to improve his brother's
prospect of a speedy solution of the case in his
favor. He insinuated, too, to his confidants that
perhaps there lay in the letter the germ of a dark
plan some day to be put to use. " Who knows,"
he would whisper, " what such a woman may be
capable of? You see how she slips from side
to side, one day for Guido, one day for her
parents. Pray God she tries no such odious plot
as she hints of here upon poor brother Guido !"

III.

THERE was in Arezzo at the time when Pompilia became the bride of Count Guido a canon of the Church named Giuseppe Caponsacchi. He was a tall and courtly priest, with a thoughtful brow, and deep, earnest, brooding eyes. His family was the oldest and noblest of the city, and he was thus free to move among the most eminent of his fellow-townsmen, their equal in birth, wealth, and social graces, and their superior in learning and loftiness of character. Like most of the prelates of his day, his devotion to the Church did not prevent him from courteous gallantries among the ladies of Arezzo, for the Church drew around her all that was fair and gay, encouraged her devotees to gather the sweets of life as well as the eternal harvest of religion.

One night, then, at the theatre, as the Canon Caponsacchi and a brother priest, the Canon Conti, cousin to Count Guido, disported themselves in a merry mood proper to the place and the play, they saw enter, stand an instant as if insensibly waiting a command, and then finally seat herself, a lady who was young, tall, and beautiful. A strangeness and a demure sadness, too, hovered about her girlish face, and it impressed Caponsacchi, he said, as when he got up

once after a matin-song and saw the workmen
break away a board or two from a rude box
lifted upon the altar. He looked again, and—
there, inside, was a Raphael!

He was staring steadily at her in his admira-
tion of her beauty and melancholy charm, when
the laughing Conti cried,—

"Look now; I'll make her return your
gaze."

He tossed a twisted paper of comfits into
her lap, then dodged behind Caponsacchi's
back, nodding and blinking the while over his
shoulder. At this she turned, looked their way
an instant, and smiled sadly at the hardihood
of the priestly gallants.

"Isn't she fair?" said Conti. "She's my new
cousin, the Lady Pompilia. The fellow lurking
there in the back of the box is Count Guido,
the old scapegrace! She's his wife. Married
three years ago. How he sulks!" And he went
on to tell all the gossip about the marriage,
and Guido's poverty and Pompilia's prospective
wealth. "Oh, to-morrow I shall suffer!" he
continued. "I was a fool to fling the sweetmeats.
To-morrow I'll invent some fib and see if I can't
find means to take you there."

That night and the next day Caponsacchi
could think of nothing else but Pompilia and
her beautiful sad face. At vespers Conti leaned

beside his seat in the choir, and part whispered, part sung to him,—

" I've louted low, but to no purpose. He saw you staring,—don't incline to know you any nearer. He'd lick your shoe, though, if you and certain others managed him warily (here a chanted verse),—but spare the wife! He beats her as it is. She's breaking her heart quite fast enough. Ah, you rogue,—there are plenty of others (another verse)—little Light-skirts yon-der,—every one knows what great dame she makes jealous. Spare the wife, though!" And then the light-hearted Conti went on with his pious chant.

The next week Caponsacchi was upbraided by his patron the Archbishop. " Young man," said the worldly-wise old prelate, " can it be true that after all your promises to be attentive to the ladies, you go and play truant all day long in church? Are you turning Molinist, forsooth?"

" Sir, what if I turned Christian?" Caponsac-chi answered quickly. " The fact is, I am some-what troubled in my mind. Arezzo is too limited a world. It is said that a priest who wants to think should go to Rome: so I'm going to Rome. I mean to live alone and look into my heart a little."

" When Lent was ended," he told his friends, " he would go to Rome."

But much was to happen before Caponsacchi
could go to Rome.

His heart was touched into something very like
love for the fair woman who had won his sympathy. He did not know, no one ever knows
when once he becomes the thrall of a genuine
passion, how little he is his own master. He
tried to cast off the alluring fancy by a renewed
application to his books; but he knew not that
the strongest symptom of the hold Pompilia's
beauty and distress had taken upon him was
this very disinclination to mingle with the
women he had until lately seen almost daily.
To read and study and ponder his religious
duty were in reality but the readiest means of
keeping before his solitary mind the image of
the ill-wedded girl.

Not long after this he was sitting in a deep
revery at twilight, with an unread book open
on his knees, thinking how his life was shaken
under him,—how great a gap lies between
what is and what should be; perhaps, too,
how far off he, a priest and celibate, was from
the sad, strange wife of Guido,—he with a
whole store of strengths eating into his heart,
while she, maybe, was in need of a finger's
help, and yet there was no way in the wide
world to stretch forth a finger to help her.
Her smile, too, when he would resolutely begin

again to scan the page, glowed through the printed lines and set him reverizing anew. In truth, Caponsacchi was a man of deep emotions though outwardly cold, and when once a feeling took possession of him it became his master and swayed his entire being.

A gentle tap came upon the chamber door, and he bade the visitor to enter. There glided in a masked and muffled woman, who laid a letter lightly on the opened book, then stood with folded arms and an impatient movement of the foot waiting for his reply.

The letter ran that she to whom he had lately thrown the comfits had a warm heart to give in exchange—and gave it,—loved him, and thus confessed it. It bade him render thanks for the gift by going that night to the side of her house where a small terrace overhung a blind and deserted street,—not the street in front. Her husband was away at his villa of Vittiano.

" And you," he asked, " what may you be ?"

" Count Guido's maid," she said ; " most of us have more than one function in his house. We all hate him, and the lady suffers so much. We pity her, and would help her at any risk,—especially since her choice is so wise a one." Here she bowed meaningly to the Canon. " What answer, sir, may I carry to the sweet Pompilia ?"

Then he took pen and wrote,—

I.—c   d   5

"No more of this! That you are indeed fair
I know, but other thoughts occupy my mind at
present. Once it would have been otherwise.
What made you, if I may ask, marry your
hideous husband? 'Twas a fault, and now you
taste the bitter fruit of it. Farewell."

"There!" he cried, exultingly, as she snatched
the note and went out, "the jealous miscreant
is crushed by his own engine. His mean soul
shows through the whole transparent trick!"
And he thought how, a month ago, he might
have been the willing dupe of the knave, perhaps have gone off to keep the appointment with
a cudgel hidden under his cloak. Now, he was
not in the mood.

But next morning brought the messenger
again, with a second letter.

"You are cruel, my Thyrsis," it said, "and
Myrtilla moans neglected, but still adores you.
Why do you not come? You must love some
one else. I hear you do. I blush to say it, but
take me too! There's a reason. I hear you mean
to go to Rome. I am wretched here; the monster
tortures me. Come carry me with you. Come!
Say you will. Do not write. I am always at my
chamber window over the terrace. Come!"

He looked keenly at the veiled messenger,
and, slyly feigning, lifted an end of her mask,
which let out a smile.

"So you gave my lines to the merry lady?" he said.

"Yes, sir. She almost kissed off the wax, and what paper was not quite kissed away she put caressingly into her bosom. Ah, she wept all night because you did not come——"

"Then wrote this second letter?" said Caponsacchi.

"Yes. She may expect you, then, at vespers?"

"What risk do we run of being discovered by Count Guido?" asked Caponsacchi.

"Why, none at all," said the messenger, eagerly. "He's away. He spends the nights at this season up at his villa. Besides, his bugbear is the Canon Conti, not you. He'd never suspect you."

The Canon wrote: "In vain do you tempt me. I am a priest, you are a wedded wife. Whatever kind of brute your husband may be, I have my scruples. Yet, should you really show a sign at the window—— And yet again, no! Best be good. My thoughts are elsewhere." "Take her that." He reached out the letter and the woman withdrew.

For a whole month after this the missives followed thick and fast. Caponsacchi was now and again overtaken in the street by the veiled messenger, and even beckoned to in the very church itself. Everywhere that a note could be lodged in his accustomed paths, there he was sure to find one. But he always answered in the same tone, always resisted and reproached the temptress.

One day, however, there was a variation of the monotonous message.

"You have gained very little by timidity. My husband has found out my love for you at length, and knows now that Cousin Conti was merely the stalking-horse for other game. My husband will stick at nothing to destroy you in Arezzo. Stand prepared to leave for Rome at once. I bade you visit me here, but now all is changed. The season is past at the villa, and he is at home. I beseech you stay away from the window! He may be posted there at any time."

Caponsacchi was piqued by such a warning to do the very thing it counselled him against. Solicited to go to the palace, he resisted with all the force of his sturdy moral nature. Exhorted to keep away, that same sturdy nature asserted its independence, stood upon its rights, and urged him on. He wrote,—

"You raise my courage, or, rather, provoke my curiosity, by your last note. Tell him he owns the palace, but not the street. That belongs to us all. If I should happen upon that way to-night, Guido will have two troubles:

first to get into a rage, then to get out again. Be cautious. At the Ave!"

At nightfall Caponsacchi went to the rendez-vous. He stood, at last, beneath the very window. Then, in place of touching the conventional lute, he cried aloud,—

"Out of your hole, Count Franceschini! Show yourself! Hear what a man thinks of a thing like you, and afterwards take what I mean to give you!"

Scarcely had he uttered the words when he turned once more, and there, at the window, framed in its black square, with a lamp in her hand, stood Pompilia. Before he could quite recover from his astonishment and assure himself that she was really flesh and blood, she had vanished.

He thought they had brought her there on some pretence of seeing a procession or a wedding-band go by, and that she was unconscious that they were using her as a snare for him. He was about to repeat his challenge to Guido, when all at once she reappeared, but this time on the terrace just above him. She could have touched his bowed head as she bent down; but he stood as if transfixed.

"You have sent me letters, sir," she said in a sad, lowered voice and with furtive glances back into the gloom. "I can neither read nor

write, and hence I have read none of them.
But the woman you gave them to, one of those
in whose power I am, has partly explained their
sense to me. She makes me listen, and reads an
odious thing,—that you, a priest, can love me,
a wife, because you once got a glimpse of my
face. I cannot, sir, believe this; but, oh! good
and true love would help me so much now. So
much, so much! Is it possible—can it be, that
you do mean what is good and true? You seem
the soul of truth, and have not been untrue to
me; I can read it in your eyes. Will you not
take me to Rome, then? When do you go?
Each minute lost is fatal. When, when? I ask."

Caponsacchi spoke fervently, but in a guarded
whisper, "Take you! It would be inhuman, un-
manly, to leave you. Yes, you shall go to your
friends to-morrow, as soon as I can arrange for
the journey. How shall I see you and help
you to escape?"

"O good and true!" she said. "Pass to-
morrow at this hour. If I am at the open
window, all is well. If I am absent, drop a
handkerchief and walk by. I shall see you
in my hiding-place, and know that everything
is ready. Return at the same time the next
evening, and the next, and so, till we can meet
and speak."

"To-morrow at this hour I will be here," said

Caponsacchi, and then she withdrew into the house.

Caponsacchi wandered away through the streets, unconscious whither he went. He was full of conflicting thoughts, of reasons for and against his promised course, of fears lest he should bring Pompilia shame by helping her as she had asked, and of fierce determination to leave her no longer at Guido's mercy.

When the gray of morning broke he found himself facing his own church of the Pieve, and felt the reproaches of his broken vows. The Church seemed to tell him to give Pompilia up; and, rising to the level of self-renunciation which she had taught him, he resolved to obey it. He went home and tried to busy himself with his books, but the effort came to naught. He saw nothing save the one black name across every white page. When sunset came he madly yearned to go to her, but he resisted. What if he were charged with cowardice and fear? He knew she would divine his true motive.

But the next evening another thought came to him and absolved him from his determination. Being a priest, he persuaded himself that he must not neglect the priest's peculiar duties. He decided to go to her as a friend, to advise her and administer spiritual comfort.

There she stood, waiting, over the terrace,

and when he drew near she spoke with hurried anxiety.

"Why, why have you made me wait two long days? We are both in the same mind: why delay? You know my need. Still, through God's pity on me, there is time! Oh, save me, save me!"

"Lady, waste no word, even to forgive me," he passionately answered. "Leave this house to-morrow night just before daybreak; there's a new moon now, and there will be no light in the early morning. Go to the Torrione, step across the broken wall, take San Clemente,— there's no other gate unguarded then,—cross to the inn beyond, and I will be there."

"If I can find the way," she said,—"but I will find it! Go now!" And then she too turned and went away.

Caponsacchi went home and made what excuses were needful to his servants. Then he put on a secular costume, and, dreaming all the way of the ecstatic minute when Pompilia should appear to him at the inn, wandered thither hours before the time appointed.

When the day began to break she came down the dark road and over the ruined wall. She was dressed all in black from head to foot. She did not speak, but glided swiftly into the carriage. Caponsacchi cried to the postilion hurriedly and under his breath.

"To Rome, then ask what you will!"

He sprang in beside her, and at last they were alone.

IV.

It was near noonday on the morning of Pompilia's flight that, as Count Guido afterwards averred upon his trial, he rose from bed, startled into consciousness by some unwonted noise among his servants, and found himself dazed and bewildered. He had a strange taste in his mouth, he said, as of a sickening opiate, and his eyes were heavy and sightless. His wife was gone from his side, and scattered about the room were a rifled clothes-chest, a money-coffer turned upside down, and several empty jewel-boxes.

"What does this mean?" he demanded sternly of his servants; but they had been drugged as well as he, and it dawned very gradually upon them that Pompilia had eloped.

"But whither, and with whom?" asked Guido.

"With whom but the Canon?" they answered in chorus, and then, with subtly-hinted ignorance and assumed despair and rage, he listened to the whole story of Caponsacchi's supposed correspondence with his wife. He could scarcely forbear a chuckle at the complete success of his plan, but he kept up the appearance of grief

with excellent effect, the more especially as
most of his servants were awake to his deceit,
and the gathered neighbors, though not perhaps
conscious of his last baseness, were nevertheless
too rejoiced at the escape of the ill-treated wife
to scan very critically the actions of the husband.

Guido got into the saddle at once, and, un-
accompanied by even a single servant, for reasons of his own, set out in pursuit of the fugitives. He found by inquiring at the earlier
stages on the Roman road, that they had a start
of eight hours at least, but he cantered steadily
on, grim and determined, his one hope being
to overtake them before they actually reached
Rome, where they would pass into the jurisdiction of the Church and so elude the full extent
of his vengeance.

Meanwhile, Caponsacchi and Pompilia had
driven with unbroken speed, scarce resting for
the bread and wine which were handed them
while the horses were changing, and never
alighting the whole day or night through until
they were within twelve hours' journey of Rome.
Then in the early morning they quickly started
off again, after the exhausted Pompilia had
received a bowl of milk from a woman at the
post-house gate; and they made no other stops
until they had reached the little white-walled

clump of houses and cypress-trees which is called Castelnuovo.

"Rome!" cried Caponsacchi, "Rome is the next stage, think! You are saved, sweet lady!"

The sky was aflame with a fierce red sunset, and when Pompilia awoke at his voice she looked about her in a bewildered way as if dazzled by the burst of color.

"No farther, no farther!" she exclaimed; "I can go no farther now!" And then she swooned and lay still and white in Caponsacchi's arms.

He bore her down from the coach and into the inn through a pitying group of grooms and idlers, and laid her on a couch within-doors. The host urged him to let her rest an hour or so, and though he dreaded to halt before they entered Rome, yet he could not refuse. He paced the passage and kept watch all night long, but she made not a single movement nor uttered even a sigh. They counselled him to have no fear, she slept so soundly; but he feared more and more as the hours sped on that something would happen to arrest their flight and prevent the fulfilment of Pompilia's dearest wish of joining her parents.

At the first touch of midnight gray in the east he was in the yard, urging the sleepy grooms to have out the coach and horses; offering them anything, all he possessed, if they would only

make haste. They worked drowsily enough in
the doubtful morning; but Caponsacchi felt that
he must awaken Pompilia even now, early as
it was, and he turned towards the steps to
ascend to her.

There, facing him in the dusk court-yard,
stood the grim and revengeful Count Guido.

" Good-morning to your priestship!" the Count
half hissed out with bitter emphasis. " Come,
the lady!—how could you leave her so soon ?
You've escaped my treatment ; you slept without drugs, I see. But I have you at last !" He
spoke now in a higher voice, and addressed the
officers he had brought in with him.

" Help, friends! Here, this is a priest, this
rascal in his smart disguise, with a sword at
his side. My runaway wife is up-stairs. Do
your duty, quick. Arrest and hold him.
There, bravo! Now come up with me and take
her."

On either side of Caponsacchi instantly stood
an officer, or he would have thrown himself,
boiling with hatred, upon the craven Count,
and plunged the sword he was so little used to
handling through his heart. The Count instinc-
tively felt this, and kept at a good arm's length
from him, even while he was in the custody of
the officers. But when Guido spoke of cap-
turing her, Caponsacchi was sobered.

"Let me lead the way," he exclaimed, "and see, when we meet, if you can detect any guilt on her face; then judge between us and him." And he pointed contemptuously towards Count Guido.

They all went up together and entered Pompilia's chamber. She lay there in the early morning sunlight as calmly as when Caponsacchi had brought her in the evening before.

Guido stalked up to the couch and pointed to the pale face on the pillow.

"Here she lies, feigning sleep! Seize her, bind her!" he said.

She started up then, aroused by the tumult of many feet and voices, and stood erect, face to face with her husband. He fell back to the alcove of the window, his black figure showing like a blot against the flood of morning light, and as he retreated, all the latent energy of her being was kindled by the sight of him.

"Away from between me and my doom!" she cried. "I am in God's hands now,—no longer yours!" And she pointed scornfully, like an angered queen, to the door, looking across her shoulder the while fearlessly into his face.

Caponsacchi made an effort to reach her side

from where he stood in the door-way, but he was pinioned fast. As he struggled the crowd pressed upon him.

"And him, too!" she cried; "you outrage him with your vile touch? But I'll save him!"

She leapt at Guido's sword, drew it, and brandished it, crying, "Die, in God's name!" but they closed about her twelve to one and disarmed her, and she lay at last, overcome and deadly white, upon the bed.

Pompilia's threatening use of the sword had intimidated Guido, and he hastened to have her taken into custody.

"You saw, you heard?" he cried again and again. "Bear witness to her disloyalty and write down her words!" Then he commanded them to carry Caponsacchi and Pompilia to the prison, meanwhile himself undertaking the search of the apartment. His fear was fast passing away now, and he began to strut about the room directing the attendants hither and thither in search of incriminating booty. Not a few winks were exchanged by the gossips who watched the work; and whispered sarcasms, levelled at Guido, clearly spoke the temper of the crowd. He was becoming a laughing-stock, revealing his true character under his temporary sense of triumph, and the sympathy of the by-standers, which had eddied in his favor at the first, was fast flowing out to Pompilia and Caponsacchi.

But the Canon now, as the officers made ready to lead him away, asserted himself, and claimed the treatment due to his station and influence.

"We are both aliens here," he said, "both noblemen of Tuscany. I am the nobler," and he proudly drew himself up to all his manly height, "and bear a name you all know and respect. I could, if I wished, refer our cause to the Ducal court, but I prefer, being the priest he tells you I am, and disguised for reasons I will reveal to my judges, to appeal to the Church I serve."

Such an appeal was lawful and could not be refused. They therefore bore the Canon and Pompilia separately to Rome to await their trial by the judicial officers of the Church.

Guido likewise, crestfallen and dishonored now, despised by those who would have avenged honor by the sword, and ridiculed by those who had seen his craven conduct at Castelnuovo, made his way to Rome, carrying such evidence against the pair as he alleged he had found at his palace at Arezzo and in the inn-room at Castelnuovo. This consisted of all the love-letters which he charged them with exchanging, and much impassioned verse written to Pompilia by the amorous Canon.

These things, with the letter written by Pompilia under his direction to his brother Paolo, Guido brought forth in the trial which promptly took place; but he was confronted by the evidence that Pompilia could neither read nor write, and by a full and convincing denial from Caponsacchi that he had ever written such letters as were produced in a hand which simulated his own. The court accepted this opposing testimony, but there had been an undoubted wrong done to Count Guido by the Canon and Pompilia, and, taking the accustomed middle course, it imposed upon Caponsacchi a nominal banishment to Civita for three years, and consigned Pompilia for a season to the convent of the Convertites at Rome.

This was not the kind of verdict that Count Guido had hoped for. His family pride and self-love had been deeply wounded by the conduct of the Comparini and by the discovery of Pompilia's base birth. But his was a vindictive nature rather than a vain one, and the miscarriage of his well-laid plot for Pompilia's undoing was more painful to him than even the injury done to the reputation of his noble house. He was welcomed, moreover, on his return to Arezzo, whither he went at the close of the trial, by an exasperating volley of sly questions and innuendoes impeaching his courage.

"What, back—you, and no wife? Left her with the Penitents, hey?" And they plied him again and again for news of Caponsacchi. "So he fired up, did he,—showed fight, and all that? And you drew also, but you didn't fight. Well, that's wiser; he's an impetuous fellow, and dangerous when he's angry."

This went on until the Count could bear it no longer. His own sense of deficiency in courage gnawed at his heart, and he longed for resolution enough to take vengeance on some of his tormentors, but he dared not venture it. His ardor cooled at the very touch of the sword-hilt.

But there was one way of harassing the real enemy and at the same time vindicating his name and house. His wife's punishment was really equivalent to an acknowledgment on the part of the court that she was deemed guilty of infidelity, and upon this ground he could readily apply for a divorce. This he promptly did, meaning by one fortunate stroke to be rid of the hated Pompilia and to secure to himself her coveted dowry, the source of all his troubles.

But the Comparini were as wary as himself. They immediately met this appeal with a counter-claim. Pompilia was made to demand a divorce from Count Guido Franceschini on the score of cruelty inflicted upon her in his household, and by himself, his mother, and his cousin, the Canon Conti.

Here was a serious dilemma. If this charge were substantiated and a divorce granted to Pompilia, the dowry, all he really desired and contended for, could never be his. He was not a brave man, nor was he a resolute one, and these accumulating ills, which to a worthier nature would have been spurs to firmness and vigorous action, were gradually unmanning him and dragging him down to the level of brutal revenge.

One more blow was to come, and it came quickly and cruelly. News now arrived at Arezzo that, Pompilia's health demanding change after three weeks' confinement in the convent, the court had consented to grant her request for transfer to some private place where she could breathe purer air and receive more wholesome food. What was more likely than that she should choose the Comparini's deep-shaded villa by the Pauline gate? There, at any rate, she became domiciled before long, under nominal imprisonment, but really free to go and come as she liked.

To the Abate Paolo in Rome, who saw in this arrangement an escape from the charges for Pompilia's maintenance which had hitherto been made upon Guido's purse, it was a welcome

piece of news. But to Guido, already goaded
to frantic hatred of the Comparini, it was a
sore and deep wound. To think that he had
driven her from his home in the company of
the man she loved, for this! To think that he
himself was responsible for her restoration to
the place of all others he wished to bar her
from! The thought was maddening, and he
brooded alone in his gloomy palace, over-
whelmed with miseries and nursing a fierce
resentment.

But now came a letter from Paolo bluntly
saying,—

"You are blessed with an heir. A child was
born to Pompilia in the Pauline villa on Wednes-
day last. This accounts for her sudden flight
from the convent. The Comparini have hidden
the child away to avoid your claims. They
mean to use it themselves: they well know its
worth to them."

This brief bit of news acted like a spark of
flint upon Guido's inflammable feelings. Vanity,
disappointment, greed, and untold rancor and
pain, burst into one consuming desire for revenge. Subtle calculation, which was with him
an innate habit, also contributed to this burning impulse. Were once Pietro, Violante, and
Pompilia out of the way and the child adjudged
his own, there would be little chance for the

wealth to elude him. The legality of Pompilia's
birth was still an undecided question, and with
herself and her parents gone, who could raise a
breath of opposition to the claims of an heir so
clearly entitled to the inheritance as Pompilia's
son?

Count Guido was at his villa in Vittiano when
the news reached him, and the sting of all his
accumulated bitterness impelled him to sudden
action. He called in his serving-people and told
them his wrongs. Though they had no reason
to love a master who was close and cruel, yet
their loyalty to his house and their sense of
justice, to which he appealed with all the art
taught him by his life of intrigue in Rome,
were aroused by his subdued yet fierce story.
He pictured his happiness with his young wife,
and dwelt on the deep injury done him by
Caponsacchi, who stole her away from him.
They scarcely waited for the end before they
began to murmur and raise threatening hands.
Their dark eyes flashed a dangerous light, and
at last they broke out in a clamor for vengeance.

"Not one of us," said a stalwart vine-dresser,
—"not one of us who dig your soil and dress
your vines but would have brained him,—the
man that tempted her. And her!—we would
have staked her too for her own share."

Then Guido fixed on the first four who caught

his eye, resolute and lusty yeomen with fresh hearts and all the young Italian fire unquenched in their veins. He chose these, filled his purse with what coin was left by the fleeing pair, put on the first rough country dress he found; then, armed with the weapons that came first to hand, the five flung out into the road and galloped on to Rome.

It was on Christmas Eve that they found themselves in the holy city, and they went directly to the Abate Paolo's house; but either because he had scented the coming trouble, with his subtle foresight, or because he had been sent away on some sudden mission for his patron Cardinal, Paolo was absent from home.

Guido and his servants, being thus foiled of lodgings and a friendly hand, wandered about the city for a week, meditating, but not daring, in the holy season, to do the deed they were bent upon. Everywhere the streets were full of festivity and mirth, and through all the church doors came constant echoes of the chant of "Peace on earth." But to Guido the refrain brought no change of heart. He knew no peace and could gain none until his enemies were destroyed. His brother's deserted house mocked him with the remembrance of past happiness and ease of heart. His whole life seemed barren of good. He saw nothing of the face of the

Holy Infant, because the face of Satan lurked always behind it. He tried to pray, but his lips murmured only hatred. The song of "Peace on earth" pealed louder and louder; but he murmured in reply, "O Lord, how long, how long to be unavenged?"

On the ninth day the strain of these conflicting purposes became unbearable, and he felt that he must act or himself perish. He started up and said, "There must be an end of this;" and then came the message, scratching in his brain like the tick of a death-watch, "One more concession, only one sure way, and but one, to determine the truth. Decide instantly; then act!"

And act he did. He called his companions together and instructed them in their parts. They were to steal through the city that night, by certain blind cuts and black turns which they had already explored, to the little suburban villa by the Pauline gate.

Accordingly, when the sun had gone down, they set out through the snow, and reached Pietro's villa without a single suspicious eye to hinder their course.

V.

WITHIN the villa life had taken on much of its old appearance since Pompilia's return.

The Comparini were still in sore need, and the gossip arising from their now notorious affairs had exposed the encroaching traces of poverty which they had taken such pains to conceal. The birth of Pompilia's child, too, had brought new cares, but it had also brought new and tenderer sentiments to the fireside, so that all else which touched upon the unfortunate marriage was allowed to rest silently in the hearts of the restored household. The worst had come and gone, they said, and they were still together to bless and comfort each other, and they asked for nothing more.

The villa by the Pauline gate, which looked gloomy enough in the dusk shade of the summer leaves, was not made much more cheerful by the bare limbs which now rose before it and partly screened it from the road. It was a place at all seasons of the year to conjure up thoughts of midnight alarms and masked robbery; and when the snow-laden winds blew about its gables it had more than ever the appearance of inviting stealthy crimes.

But the interior was cheerful enough, whatever the outside might suggest. Around the blazing hearth the family group sat comfortably bending in to the glow of the wood and talked of Pompilia's boy, what he should do and be when he was grown up, and what name he should

bear,—Pompilia said Gaetano,—and a thousand
fancies more which Pompilia set on foot, and
which the old couple spun eagerly and endlessly
out.

They had given Pompilia each an arm to lead
her about from the couch to the fireside, and
now they laughed as she lay safe in her seat,
predicting how, one day, she should have a
strong son's arm to help her in her need. Then
they all laughed again in quiet contentment and
wished one another once more a happy New
Year.

But Pietro still dwelt a little on his wrongs
and his slender purse, and occasionally he would
break forth with half a sigh for the old friends
and old habits.

" Our cause is gained," he said, " but we will
avoid the city now,—no more parade and feast-
ing, and all that. We'll go to the other villa
still farther off, where we can watch the boy
grow. Ah, well, one or two friends may still
hunt us up,—and I'll have a flask of the old
sort for them, never fear."

" You chatter like a crow," said Violante.
" Pompilia's tired now and must go to bed.
Enough for the first day, a little more to-morrow, and the next she can begin to knit. I've
spun wool enough; see, child!" And she held
up the bulky skeins.

The next day about noon Pietro went out. He was so happy, and talked so much, that Violante pushed him forth into the cold.

"So much to see in the churches," she said. "Swathe your throat three times round, and above all beware of the slippery ways, and bring us all the news by supper-time."

He came back late and laid by his cloak, staff, and hat. They were powdered thick with snow, and Pompilia and Violante laughed at them, as he rolled out a great ashen log upon the hearth and bade Violante treat to a flask in return for his obedience. Ay, he had gone faithfully through the seven churches, and there was none to his mind like old San Giovanni.

"There's the fold," he said, "and the sheep, in a flock, as big as cats! And such a shepherd, —half life-size,—he starts up and hears the angel——"

Then at the door there came a tap. They all started up together. Violante went over, and, without lifting the latch, called,—

"Who's there?"

She stood listening.

After a moment's silence some one on the other side answered,—

"Giuseppe Caponsacchi."

It was Guido who had answered As the five stealthy figures stole up to the villa door, they

saw the warm light stream through the cracks,
and felt the sense of life only an inch or two
within. Some angel must have whispered Guido
to give his victims one more chance, for he bade
the others stand aside, and himself knocked at
the door. As Violante spoke, he resolved to
make a last trial of Pompilia. If the door
opened to Caponsacchi's name, her guilt was
proven and his deed would be justified. Perhaps, too, he welcomed, even at this extremity,
any excuse which would afford him an oppor-
tunity for retreat.

He called the name, therefore, and the door
was promptly opened. Violante stood with
welcoming hands upon the threshold. Pompilia
had risen from her chair, and her hands, joy-
ously clasped, told how eager she was to see her
rescuer. Old Pietro turned half around from
the fire with a dubious look. He scented new
trouble in this last intrusion.

There was a pause outside, and Violante was
surprised to see three or four dark figures, who
drew farther into the gloom as she advanced to
the step. Then, presently, one broke from the
rest and strode boldly forward. It was Guido,
whose hatred had overcome his cowardice. In
an instant and without warning he sprang upon
her, and she fell across the door-way wounded
with a dagger-thrust. He stepped over her

and plunged into the room, and then the rest
entered and threw themselves upon old Pietro
and Pompilia.

When all was done, the five dark figures
emerged from the door-way and filed noiselessly
out through the garden into the high-road. The
snow on the ground muffled their tread, and
they followed their leader swiftly and without
a word up the deserted road.

But the noises within had aroused the neighbors, and before the murderers were well out
of sight friends from the near-by mill and
grange came flocking in to see what had happened. They were followed promptly by the
Public Force, the Head of which, tracking the
footprints in the snow, was soon out in hot
pursuit of the fugitives.

Guido and his men had the start and chose
their own direction, and they travelled rapidly,
notwithstanding the condition of the wintry
road. But, in spite of his craftiness and his
week of calculating preparation, Guido had
neglected to provide himself with the necessary
passes for travelling by post. He boldly demanded horses from the postmaster, and dis-
creetly slid a ducat into his palm, whispering
how he, the Count, and his four knaves had just
been mauling an enemy whose kindred might

prove troublesome : they wanted horses in a
hurry.   But the postmaster refused unless the
Count could show him the Permission.   Guido
whispered again, this time that he was a Duke,
not a Count, that the dead man was a Jew.
But he found he was dealing with perhaps the
one scrupulous fellow in all Rome.   The Count
was without a hat and was splashed with blood.
The determined postmaster finally put by his
bribe and insisted on the rules of the road.

"Where is the seal of the Roman Police?
You might have had it half an hour ago for the
asking."

"Lost," said Guido.

"Get another, then, or you get no horses
here."   And he stood stubbornly blocking their
passage in the midst of the road.

But he dared not use force.   He was only one
to a grim and menacing band of five.   They
scowled fiercely at him and strode past into
the darkness.   There was no alternative but to
travel afoot, and this they did for twenty miles,
panting and plunging on the miry road, through
the bleak, open country, through the still and
lightless villages by the way, and on as far as
Baccano.

The rough beginning of the journey taxed the
strength of the younger men, but much more
that of Count Guido, who was overweary in

soul and flesh, for he had to think as well as act. When they had reached Baccano, a town this side of the boundary of Tuscany and still within the jurisdiction of Rome, they found shelter in an outlying grange. They had hoped to set foot on Tuscan soil before resting, and thus they might have bidden defiance to the severity of Roman law; yet they sank down exhausted almost within sight of the border.

But the tireless officer of the Roman Force had followed them unceasingly through the night, and tracked them in the early morning to the deserted grange at Baccano.

There they lay in a lifeless heap, one across the other, deaf, dumb, and blind through the fatigues and burning passions of their night's work. They were red from head to heel, and their weapons bespoke the loathsome work they had been used in.

When at last he was aroused by the voices and the rough handling of the officers, Guido put on a bold front and furiously demanded to know why he was thus disturbed, what right they had to dog the steps of a stranger and his servants in Rome?

"What am I charged with?" he indignantly cried. "Who is my accuser?"

"Why, naturally, your wife," was the grim answer.

" My wife!"

The terrible truth flashed on him. She was still alive; she had seen and known him at the villa.

Then, realizing his danger, his craven heart sank within him. His cowardly nature lost its courage with its bravado. He fell heavily from the horse on which they had set him for the journey back to Rome. He was quickly restored and remounted, and then the five pinioned criminals were carried to the city and thrown into prison. And that same day old Pietro and Violante were laid by the altar in San Lorenzo church.

Yet for four days did Pompilia linger in the Roman hospital. She was cruelly wounded by a hand which hated deeply and thirsted for her life. She had been left for dead on the villa floor only after the murderers had listened at her still heart and tested her breathless lips. Guido had held her lovely head up by the long silken hair while his accomplices watched for the signs of life. Then, when he was convinced that she was dead,—she whom he cursed from his heart as the source of all his ills,—he cast her away from him, and hurried out to gain the protection of his Tuscan home.

Unconscious, she had lain for a long time, but not dead; and when the doctors came in they

found the life still eddying through her muti-
lated limbs. She was carried to the hospital,
and there told her story, her whole life as she
had known it, to the good friar Don Celestine.

"All these things are true," she feebly said.
"You must remember them, because time flies.
The surgeon cared for me and counted my
wounds,—twenty-two dagger-wounds, five of
them deadly; but I do not suffer much. He
says I cannot live beyond to-night."

Then in a half-whisper, while the patient friar
leaned down to her pillow, she told him her
pitiful tale. She dwelt much upon the bright
spots in her dark life, on the birth of her son
Gaetano, on the tenderness and care of Caponsacchi, and on the love of her old parents, whom
she had been so happy to join again after the
cruel life at Arezzo. She said little about Count
Guido, neither accusing nor blaming him. Hers
was a wistful and pathetic narrative of sim-
plicity and innocence that had been deceived,
but she kept her sweet forbearance to the end,
and made no accusations against those who had
wronged her. Yet when she came to speak, at
the last, about her child, she was sure, she said,
that he could be only his mother's, born solely
of love, not of hate.

"Let us leave God alone," she murmured.
"He will explain, in good time, what I only feel

now. I cannot say the things I would. It
seems impossible to-day. But I shall be righted
hereafter. Many things are never explained,
but just known."

Then, as if faint with her effort to tell all, she
sank into quietness. But it was only momen-
tary. Her struggling spirit broke through the
flesh's weariness, and she whispered tranquilly,
but with a new lustre in her eyes,

"There is more yet. My last breath must be
true. He is still here in the world. It is now,
when I am like to leave, that I feel most the
old sensations. Again the face and eyes, and
the heart of my one friend, with its immeas-
urable love! My only friend, all my own, who
put his breast between me and the spears. No
work that is begun will, I think, ever pause for
death. Love will be more and more helpful to
me in the coming course. Tell him that if I
seem without him now, that's the world's in-
sight. Oh, he understands! He is at Civita,—
the world is holding us apart again. Tell him
it was his name I sprang to when the knock
came at the door. It is through such souls as
his that God shows us enough of his light to
rise by."

She sank back upon her pillow, wan and still.
The fire had burnt out the shell which held it,
They covered her and paced sadly away.

Then Pompilia was carried to San Lorenzo church and laid on the altar beside Pietro and Violante, who had wronged her greatly through loving her greatly.

But with Count Guido Franceschini it fared otherwise. He and his four peasant accomplices were taken before the earthly judges of Rome, and were by them condemned to pass from the scaffold before a higher tribunal.

On the day appointed they were dragged in open carts through the crowded streets to the Place of the People, where a holiday throng had gathered to see the end of a noble convict. There, as had been decreed, Guido suffered death upon the block, and his four knaves were hung, two on each side of him.

Human justice was at last appeased for the crime done at the villa by the Pauline gate.

I.—*f*

THE PRINCESS.

ALFRED, LORD TENNYSON.

THE PRINCESS.

I.

In a land under the Northern star there lived once a Prince of royal blood, who was very fair of face, and wore long yellow ringlets in token of his birth in the country of the year-long snow. He was, though, of an amorous temper and fond of romantic adventure, and if these traits fitted ill with his Norland blue eyes and flaxen hair, they made him none the less noble, but threw about him a subtler charm than belonged to his hardier kinsfolk.

Now, there was an ancient legend in the house of this Prince that some sorcerer, who was burnt by a far-off ancestor because he cast no shadow, had foretold when he died that none of all that royal lineage should know shadow from substance, and that at last one should come to fight with shadows and should fall in the fray.

Such was the story the Prince's mother had taught him at her knee; and in good truth

waking dreams had always been, more or less,
the prevailing affection of the house. The Prince
himself had, as he grew up, weird seizures. On
a sudden in the daylight and in the very midst
of his companions—even while he walked and
talked as he was accustomed to do—he seemed
to move in a world of ghosts and feel like the
mere shadow of a dream. The great court
physician nodded gravely over such a symptom
and stroked his beard in meditation, then he
muttered "catalepsy" or some such thing, and
did nothing at all to cure the malady.

The Prince's mother was much troubled by
his seizures and said a thousand prayers for his
recovery, for she was as mild as a saint and
half canonized by her subjects, so gracious and
tender was she in all things. But the King, his
father, thought a king should be all a king. He
cared little for the love of his royal household,
but held his sceptre like a school-master's rod,
the scourge of offenders, whom with his long
hands reached forth he picked out from the
mass of his people for austere judgment.

It chanced, while the Prince was still but a
tender youth, that he was betrothed to a neigh-
boring Princess; and she was proxy-wedded to
him with a calf, as the custom in that land was,
at eight years old. From time to time rumors
of her beauty came to the Northern court from

the South, where she dwelt, and also came gossip
about her well-knit and comely brothers, who
were youths of prowess in the field of sport
and fight. The Prince still wore her picture
hanging at his heart, and beside it a single dark
tress of her hair, and all about these tokens his
thoughts would constantly hover, like a swarm
of bees about its queen.

But the time drew near when the real wedding should take place between the Prince and
his betrothed bride; and his father the King
sent ambassadors, bearing gifts of furs and
jewels, to bring her back. They went their
way, and returned at the allotted time carrying
a wondrous piece of tapestry with them as an
offering to the King, but not the Princess. The
answer from the South was as vague as the
wind. They saw the King, her father; he took
the gifts, he acknowledged there was a compact
of marriage, all that was true; but then she
had a will of her own,—was he to blame for
that?—and also maiden fancies of an unusual
kind,—liked to live alone among her women;
and, in short, he was certain she would not wed.

The Prince stood by the throne in the presence-
room as this message was delivered, and with him
were his two friends, Cyril, a gentleman of
broken fortunes, due to his father's waste, but
a merry and revelling companion, and Florian,

the Prince's bosom comrade, almost his half
self, for they were never apart.

While the returned ambassadors spoke, the
Prince watched his father's face and saw it
grow long and troubled, then threatening and
wrathful. The King started to his feet and tore
the letter from his Southern ally into atoms, and
these he cast down angrily, and then rent through
with one blow the beautiful tapestry, his royal
gift. At last he swore that he would send a hundred thousand men and bring the Princess in a
whirlwind. Then he turned to his war-captains
and appeased his wrath in martial talk.

But at last the Prince spoke up: "Let me go,
father. Perhaps some mistake has been made.
I cannot believe that such a king, one whom
everybody praises for fairness and kindness,
should send back such an answer; or maybe if
I saw the Princess I should not care for her
and should repent my bargain."

And Florian said, "I have a sister there, too,
an attendant on the Princess. She married a
nobleman of that country, who died lately and
left her the lady of three castles. Through her
we might do much to mend matters."

"Take me, too," whispered Cyril. "What if
you have a seizure there in a strange land?
You'll need a trusty friend, and I'll be that.
I'm rusting out here in idleness."

" No !" roared the irate King, " you shall not !
We ourself will crush her pretty maiden fancies
in these iron gauntlets ! Break up the council !"

And then the company scattered, in some
dread of the royal rage ; but the Prince went
forth into the woods that circled the town, and,
finding a still place, pulled out the Princess's
likeness and laid it on the flowers beside his
bending elbow. As he gazed on the sweet face
of his betrothed he began to wonder what were
her strange fancies and why she wanted to break
her troth. The lips surely looked a trifle proud
and disdainful ; but while he meditated a wind
came up from the south and shook all the leaves
overhead together, and a voice seemed to come
from them saying, " Follow, follow, and thou
shalt win."

Then before the moon grew full, for it was
now but a slender crescent, he stole from court
with Cyril and Florian, and crept through the
town, dreading each moment to hear the hue
and cry of his father hallooing at his back.
But all was quiet enough, and they dropped over
the bastioned walls like spiders and fled away,
and reached the frontier before they were
missed. They crossed then to a livelier country, and so, through farms and vineyards and
tracts of green wilderness, they gained the King's
city, where amid its circling towers arose the

imperial palace, and thither they went and found the King.

His name was Gama. He had a small cracked voice and but little dignity, but his smile was bland enough and drove his old cheeks into wrinkling lines. He looked in truth not much like a king, but he was royal in his treatment of the visitors, and for three whole days they feasted in his palace. Then on the fourth day they told him, mellowed with wine and hearty with good cheer, why they had come, and of the Prince's desire to see his betrothed.

"You do us great honor, Prince," he said. "We remember love ourself in far-away youth. Yes, we made a compact with your father—a kind of ceremony—I think"—and he placed one musing finger on his brow—"I think it was the summer our olives failed. Hem! I would you had her, Prince. But there was a pair of widows here, Lady Psyche and Lady Blanche, who fed her with all sorts of theories, in place and out, always proving to their own satisfaction that women are the equal of men. They harped on the subject forever; all our banquets rang with it; even the dancers broke up into knots to discuss it. Nothing but this one theme from morning till night. My very ears grew hot to hear them at it! Heigh-ho! my daughter said knowledge was the all in all. As children they

had only existed; they must now leave off
being children, cease merely to exist, and be
women. Then she wrote awful odes and dismal
lyrics and made rhymed prophecies of change
and all that. And they sang these things, sirs,
and *I* went away and sought quiet, but her
women called them masterpieces. They cer-
tainly mastered me! Well, at last she came
and begged a boon of me. Would I give her
my summer palace up by your father's frontier?
I said no, of course, but she wheedled it out of
me, and she and her maidens went there and
founded a University for their sex alone. We
know no more about it than this: they see no
men,—not even her brother Arac, nor the twins,
though they look upon her as a paragon. Well,
I was loath to breed trouble, but since you think
me bound in some sort by my compact, as no
doubt I am, why, if you wish it, I can give you
letters to her. But I don't think your chance of
seeing her is worth much."

The Prince was somewhat nettled by such
cool disregard of a solemn compact, but he
was chafing now to get a glimpse of his bride,
and he took the letters and rode forth with
his friends to the northward.

At last, after a long day's ride, they looked off
from a sloping hill-side and saw a rustic town,
which they presently entered at evening, and

found it a fair place set in the crescent of a winding river. There they found an old hostel, and called the landlord into council upon their adventure. They plied him with his own richest wines, and showed him the King's letters, which he touched with reverence.

The landlord declared it was against all rules for any man to go to the University, but under the seductive touch of the wine and out of respect for the royal sign-manual he relented at last.

"Well, if the King has given the letters," he said, "I am not bound to speak. The King's a law unto himself, and he'll bear me out if I obey his behests. But," he added, with a sly wink,—"but no doubt you would make it worth my while? She passed this way once," he chattered on, "and I heard her speak. How she scared me! Oh, I never saw the like! She looked as grand and as grave as doomsday. But I reverence her too,—she's my liege-lady, your honors; and I always make a point to use mares for the posting, and my daughter and the housemaids I make do for boys. Why, the land all about is tilled by women,—and the swine are all sows, too; and all the dogs——"

But while the portly host jested and laughed in this wise, a thought struck the Prince, which he acted on instantly. Remembering how he

and Florian and Cyril had once taken the parts
of nymphs and goddesses in a masque at his
father's court, he now sent the landlord out to
buy female apparel for all three, and very soon
mine host returned laden with gowns and furbe-
lows and himself shaken with an ill-suppressed
mirth. He helped to lace the trio up in the
maidenly garb, and they gave him a costly bribe
to keep silence; then they mounted their steeds
and ventured boldly into the domain of the
Princess.

They followed the winding course of the river
as they had been directed to do, and at midnight
began to see the far-off college-lights glittering
like fire-flies in a copse. Then they passed an
arch, above which rose a statue of a woman
with wings, riding four winged horses, and they
could make out in the deep shadow that some
inscription ran along the front, but could not
read it. Farther on they came into a little
street of gardens and houses, where the noise of
clocks and chimes was deafening, so many were
there in the place. Fountains, too, spouted up
here and there amid the flowers, and the song
of nightingales filled up all the intervals of
sound.

Before them now rose a bust of Pallas, between two lamps blazoned like Heaven and
Earth and resting above an open entry. Riding

in thither, they called for attendance, and a
lusty hostleress, followed by a stable-wench,
came running out and helped them down. Then
a buxom hostess stepped forth, and led them
into their rooms, which looked out on a pillared
porch deeply based in laurel-leaves.

They questioned her about the college, and
asked who were tutors.

" Lady Blanche and Lady Pysche," she said.

The three candidates cried in one voice, " We
are hers!"

Then the Prince sat down and wrote in a
slanted hand like a woman,—

"Three ladies of the Northern empire pray
Your Highness to enroll them in your college as
the Lady Psyche's pupils."

He sealed and gave this letter to the land-
lady, to be sent at dawn, and then the three
companions went to bed and dreamed of the
adventures to be.

II.

EARLY in the morning the College Portress
came to the place where the Prince and his
friends were resting, and brought them Aca-
demic silks of lilac color, with silken hoods and
girdles of gold. They put these on without
parley, and then the Portress, courtesying her
obeisance, told them that the Princess Ida

waited. They followed her through a laurel-grown porch, and came forth into a marble court supported with classic friezes and covered with ample awnings hung up between the pillars. A fountain played in the midst, circled by the Muses and Graces in groups of three, and here and there scattered about on the lattice edges lay a book or lute. They passed on, and ascended a flight of stairs into a great hall.

There, with two tame leopards couched near her throne, sat the Princess at a table filled with volumes and loose papers. In the Prince's eyes she seemed the sum of all beauty, as fair indeed as an inhabitant of some planet nearer to the sun than ours. Such eyes, so much grace and power looking down from her arched brows, he had never beheld until now, and with every turn she made her perfection lived through her to the tips of her long hands and to her very feet.

She rose to her full height, and said, "We give you welcome. Not without some glory to ourselves have you come to us, the first-fruits of stranger lands. Hereafter in the voice which circles around the grave you will rank nobly, mingled in fame with me." Then, noticing them more closely, she exclaimed,—

"But are the ladies of your land all so tall?"

"We of the court," said Cyril.

"From the court," she answered. "Then you know the Prince?"

"The climax of his age! Indeed yes, your Highness; and as though there were but one rose in the whole world, so he worships you."

"We scarcely expected to hear such barren speech in our own hall," she said. "This light kind of coin is current among men, but not with us. Your escape from the bookless desert would seem to argue love of knowledge, but your language proves you still a child. Indeed, we dream not of the Prince. When we set our hand to this great work we purposed never to wed. You likewise, ladies, will do well, in entering here, to cast away such tricks as make you the toys of men."

After this harangue the Prince and his fellow-candidates seemed much abashed and looked steadily down at the matting. Then an officer arose and read the statutes of the foundation, which declared that for three years no undergraduate could correspond with home, or cross the boundary, or speak with a man. These and a score of others the new scholars hastily subscribed to, and they were then received without further ceremony into the college.

"Now," said the Princess, admonishingly, "you are one with us. But you are still green wood. See to it that you do not warp."

Then she led them with majestic movements into the hall beyond, and showed them one by one the statues of ancient queens and noble women of old which stood there. She turned as they passed out through the door and spoke words of counsel to them, exhorting them to live worthy lives and to work out their freedom from masculine thraldom. At last she dismissed them and bade them go to the Lady Psyche's class-room, where all those newly arrived were gathered for their first lecture.

Back they went across the sylvan court-yard and found the room, and took their seats with the throng of pupils already clustered at the long forms. The teacher herself sat erect behind an elevated desk. She was a sharp-eyed brunette, alert and well moulded, and perhaps on the hither side of twenty years. At her left slept her infant, Aglaïa, wrapped in embroidered draperies. She glanced keenly at the Prince and his companions as they entered, and not a gesture or movement of theirs escaped her. After a searching look at her face, Florian whispered,—

"By Heaven, my sister!"

"Comely, too, by all that's fair," said Cyril.

"Oh, hush, hush!" urged the Prince, and she began to speak.

"This universe was at one time nothing but

liquid flame. Then the star tides set in towards
the centre of chaos and formed suns. These
cast off the planets. Then came monsters, and
at last man." Here she proceeded to take a
bird's-eye view of the whole earth's past history,
and, at last, drifted from this into a prophecy
of the future, when, everywhere, there would
be two heads in council, two by the hearth,
two in commerce, two in science and art and
poetry.

Thus after a long harangue she ended, and
the class began to depart, but she beckoned to
the Prince and his friends to come near to
her desk. They moved forward as she directed, and she addressed some words to them
in praise of the worthy course they had chosen.

But her voice faltered, after a little speech,
and she seemed no longer able to play her part.
She fairly broke down at last, and cried,—

"My brother!"

"Well, my sister?" demurely said Florian.

"Oh, what do you mean by coming here?
And in this dress? And who are these——
Wolves in the fold! The Lord be gracious to
me! a plot, a plot, a plot! It will ruin all!"

"No plot, no plot," he answered.

"Wretched boy! did you not see the inscription above the gate,—LET NO MAN ENTER IN ON
PAIN OF DEATH?"

"And if I had," said Florian, "I would not have believed you as savage as you seem."

"But you will find it true," she said. "You may jest if you choose; but it's ill jesting with edge-tools."

"Very well, then, kill me, and nail me to the door like a weasel for a warning! Bury me by the gate, and write above me,—

'*Here lies a brother by a sister slain,*
All for the common good of womankind.'"

"Let me be slain, too," said Cyril. "I have seen the Lady Psyche and am content to die."

Then said the Prince, motioning the others to silence,—

"Notwithstanding my disguise, madam, I love the truth. Hear it, then, and in me behold your countryman, the Prince, affianced years ago to the Lady Ida. Because she is here, and because there was no other way to come hither, I have ventured to come thus."

"Oh, sir, my Prince!" said the Lady Psyche, "I have no country any more, or if I have, it is only this. But, truly, I have none, none at all! Affianced, sir, you say? Nothing that speaks of love must be breathed within this vestal limit. And how should I, who am sworn to obey in all things, bid you stay here and live? The thunderbolt hangs silent; but, believe me, it will fall anon."

" Hold !" cried the Prince, as she moved away. " What if the inscription speaks truly, and we are put to death,—what follows ? War, and all your precious work marred ; and your Academy, whichever side conquers, destroyed !"

" Let the Princess judge of that," she said. " And now farewell, sir." And to Florian and Cyril she made a pitiful adieu, and then, " I shudder for your fate, but I am bound in duty to go."

Before she had quite passed from them the Prince spoke, and she turned to listen.

" Are you," he said, " that Lady Psyche, the fifth in line from old Florian, whose portrait hangs in our palace showing him astride my fallen grandsire as he defended him when all else had fled ? We point to it even to this day and say, the loyalty of Florian has not grown cold, but runs warm among us in kindred veins."

" Are you that Psyche with whom I romped in childhood?" pleaded Florian. " Are you the same that bound my brow and smoothed my pillow in sickness and told me pleasant tales and read the pain away into happy dreams ? Are you the brother and sister in one whom I loved of old ? You *were*, perhaps, but what are you now ?"

" You are that Psyche," followed Cyril, " for

whom I would forever be what I seem,—a woman, so that I might sit at your feet and glean wisdom."

Then again each in turn pleaded with her, appealed to her heart, and to her love of the land which bore her, and to her affection for her babe; so that at last, moved and vexed, she cried,—

"Out upon it! peace! And why, then, should I not play the Spartan mother? why should I not be the Brutus of my sex? You call him great because he made sacrifice of self to the common good. What of me? Shall I, on whom the emancipation of half the world rests,—shall I do less? Shall I hesitate to give up a Prince, and a brother?" But she softened visibly at the thought, and went on more calmly: "Yet perhaps it would be better if I yielded something, and I will on one condition: you must promise—otherwise you perish—to slip away to-day, or at most to-morrow, and I will tell the Head that you were too barbarous,—could not be taught; you might have brought shame upon us, and we are lucky to be rid of you. Promise, and all shall be well."

There was no alternative, so the three intruders promised what she asked, and she, like a wild creature newly caged, paced to and fro about the room, struggling with her emotions. At last she paused by Florian and held out her hands; taking both of his in a fervent grasp. Smiling faintly, she said, "I knew you, dear Florian, from the first,—the very first. You have grown, but you have not altered, no, not the least. I am very glad, yet very sad, to see you, my brother. Pardon my threats and harshness; it was duty that spoke, not I. And our mother, tell me, is she well?"

With that she reached up and kissed his forehead, and then clung about him with sisterly affection, and between them, from old veins of memory, began to flow sweet household talk and pensive allusions to the past, which moistened the tender Psyche's eyes.

But while they stood thus in happy forgetfulness, there came a voice at the door:

"Here is a message from the Lady Blanche."

Psyche started and looked up. It was the Lady Blanche's daughter Melissa, who stood waiting in timid consciousness of her intrusion. She was a rosy blonde, dressed in a college gown of yellow silk, and she looked like a slender daffadilly as she gazed with timid eyes into the room.

"You, Melissa?" exclaimed Psyche. "You heard us, then?"

"Oh, pardon," faltered Melissa. "I did hear; I could not help it. I did not wish to. But, dearest lady, pray do not fear me. I will do nothing to harm these gallant gentlemen."

"I trust you, Melissa," said Psyche, "for we were always friends. But your mother, child! —what if she heard? Do not let your prudence sleep a wink. It would ruin all!"

"You need not fear me," said Melissa. "I would not tell, not even for power to answer all that Sheba asked of Solomon."

"Be it so," said Psyche; and then turning to the conspirators, "Go, now," she said; "we have already been too long together. Draw your hoods close about your faces. Speak little. Do not mix with the rest, and keep your promise."

They started to go, but Cyril took up Psyche's child and blew out his cheeks like a trumpeter to amuse it. The lady smiled, and the baby pushed forth her fat hand against his face and laughed, and when he set her down they went out.

Half the long day they wandered about the stately theatres of the college. They sat in each one in turn, and heard the grave professors discourse on all things human and superhuman, until they were quite gorged with knowledge, and the Prince said,—

"Why, after all, they do this as well as we do."

"They hunt old trails," said Cyril, "but never advance; women never can."

"Ungracious!" exclaimed Florian, "did you

learn no more than that from Psyche? You
told her a heap of trash, at any rate. It quite
made me sick."

"Oh, trash! Well, but there was a reason.
She made me wise in one way, truly. A thousand hearts lie fallow here and a thousand baby
Loves go flitting about with headless arrows.
Well, the bigger boy, Cupid himself, has struck
me; and, after all, do I chase shadow or substance? There's no sorcerer's malison upon me,
as there is upon His Highness here. I know a
shadow when I see it. Are castles shadows,
think you? Is she herself a shadow in all her
loveliness? Why, then, should those three castles not help to patch my tattered coat? But
hark, there's the bell for dinner!" And the ad-
venturers went into the great hall and found
places at the table among the long rows of fair
students, who chattered in deepest terms of
science and philosophy throughout the long
meal.

When the solemn grace was over the Prince
and his friends went forth into the gardens, but
sat apart in muffled silence, save that Melissa
came now and again to rally them, while the
rest played at ball, or gossiped by the fountain's
edge, or opened books and paced to and fro
upon the smooth sod.

At last the chapel-bell called to evening service, and the Prince and his fellows mixed with the six hundred maidens, clad all in purest white, and passed in where the great organ played solemn hymns, the work of the Lady Ida in verse and melody, made to call down a blessing on her labors.

III.

When the morning came the three trespassers carefully dressed one another and descended to the courts, which lay shadowed and dewy below their windows. They were idly standing beside the fountain, watching the bubbles dance and break, when Melissa approached them, pale with tears and loss of sleep.

"Fly, fly," she whispered, "while there's still time! My mother knows all."

"What?" said the Prince, startled by the news.

"It was my fault. Oh, don't blame me! I could not help it. She divined it, drew it from me. It is all because of her jealousy of the Lady Psyche. She said you looked more like men than like women, and laughed at Lady Psyche's countrywomen. And I——"

"You blushed," said Cyril.

"Yes, yes, I blushed, and then she knew, and said, 'Why—these—*are*—men—and you know it! And *she* knows, too, and conceals it.' And now she has gone to the Princess, and Lady

Psyche will be crushed. But there is still hope for you if you fly at once. Oh, pardon me, say you pardon me, before you go!"

"But who asks pardon for a blush, my sweet Melissa?" said Cyril. "Go to, I'll straighten all out, never fear. I must see this Lady Blanche and soften her humor." And he went away to find Melissa's mother.

Then Florian asked the fair girl whence the feud between the right and left, her mother's and his sister's halves of the college, had grown, and she told him how the Lady Psyche had come from the North and won from Lady Blanche the heart of the Princess, and how the Lady Psyche and the Lady Ida were boon friends, and for this her mother called the Lady Psyche plagiarist, and hated her. When she had said all this, Melissa darted away, and Florian murmured to the Prince as he gazed after her,—

"Surely, an open-hearted girl. I think if I could ever come to love, I'd choose her rather than your stately Princess, crammed with pride and musty learning."

"Well, let the crane chatter about the crane and the dove about the dove," said the Prince. "Every man to his liking. For me, the Princess! If she errs, why, she does it nobly, that you must allow."

So disputing, they paced across the court, and reached the terrace which ran along its northern front. There they leaned upon the balusters, gazing out upon the wide and fair landscape below them. Thither came Cyril, in a little while, yawning.

"Oh, what a task!" he cried. "No fighting shadows,—a real Amazon!"

"And what success?" asked the Prince.

"She was hard as flint," replied Cyril, "with a malignant light in her green eyes. I was courteous and conciliatory, but to no purpose. Who were we? she asked. I made no concealment,—told her all, and dwelt upon your betrothal to the Princess. But she answered that I talked astray; it was untrue. I appealed to her mercy, to her love for Melissa, who might come to harm for concealing her knowledge of us; but she still repulsed me. At last I plied her with an offer which tempted: 'Would she accept in our kingdom the headship of another college, where she should reign supreme, not fall to third place, as here?' This moved her. She is to give us her answer to-day, and meantime will not betray us."

Here they were interrupted by a messenger from the Head, who announced that the Princess intended to ride forth that afternoon in order to take the dip of certain northern strata, and

invited them to go with her. They would find
the land worth seeing, said the maiden, and
she pointed to the hills beyond, rising at the
edges of the vale, where, she told them, was a
water-fall.

When the hour had arrived, the Prince and
his friends went to the porch where the Lady
Ida stood among her pupils, higher by a head
than any of them. She leaned against a pillar,
and supported her foot upon the back of one
of her tame leopards. The lithe animal rolled
over kitten-like and pawed at her sandal, but
she did not notice it.

The Prince drew near and gazed raptly at
her. Then, on a sudden, his strange seizure
came upon him, and the Princess and all her
maidens seemed a hollow show and he himself
the very shadow of a dream. But yet his heart
beat fast with passion, and as she glanced, once,
at him, he sighed in spite of himself and felt a
longing to kneel at her feet.

But at last the gay company of girls all got to
horse and rode forth in a long retinue, following
the winding course of the river as it narrowed
between the hills.

The Prince rode beside the Lady Ida.

"We trust you thought us not overharsh with
your companion yesterday," she said to him.
"We were loath to speak so."

"No, not to her," he answered, "but to him of whom you spoke."

"Again?" she cried. "Are you envoys from him to me? But, as you are a stranger, we will give you license. Speak this once, and then no more of the subject."

The disguised Prince stammered that he knew him,—that the King expected her to wed his son; and then he burst out, "Indeed, you seem all the Prince prefigured but could not see. Surely if you keep your purpose he will be driven to despair,—even to death."

"Poor boy," she said, "can he not read, or forget his worship in ball or quoits? Does he take no delight in martial exercise? Why, he's no better than a silly girl to nurse his blind ideal till it enslaves him so." Then she paused, and added, haughtily, "As to precontracts, we move at no man's nod. Like noble Vashti, we keep our state and leave the brawling King at Shushan."

But the Prince said, "You grant me license to speak. May I use it freely? Think of the future. You leave your work hereafter to feebler hands that overthrow all you have reared. May you not miss in this wise what every woman counts her due,—love, children, happiness?"

"Peace, you young savage!" she exclaimed, astonished at the girl's hardihood. "You are

overbold; we are not accustomed to be talked
to thus by our own pupils. Yet as for children,"
she added in a softer voice, " we like them well;
would they grew everywhere like wild-flowers!
But children die; and let me tell you, girl, babble as you please, great deeds cannot die."

The Prince made no answer. He was over-
awed by her fierce outburst, and wondered
within himself if she might ever be won.

She seemed to interpret his thoughts, and
spoke again:

" We no doubt appear a kind of monster in
your eyes; but we are used to that, for women
have been so long cramped under a worse than
South-Sea taboo that they cannot guess how
much their welfare has become a passion with
us."

She bowed then, as if to veil a tear that
came in spite of herself. The Prince looked far
ahead the while, and saw that they had arrived
where the river sloped to the cataract of which
the messenger had spoken. The trees were
above them, and below the plunging waters,
which foamed over a mass of great boulders
with an unceasing roar. There, too, beside the
water, stuck out the bones of some vast monster
that had lived before the advent of man. The
Princess gazed at the skeleton awhile, then
said,—

"As those rude bones are to us, so are we to the woman that is to be."

"Dare we dream of the power that wrought us as of the workman who betters with practice?" said the Prince.

"How!" she cried, "you love metaphysics? Read, then, and win the prize!" And she warmed to the subject, and told him all her plans, and described to him the device carven on the brooch which he would gain by winning. They talked on from point to point of the college curriculum. The Prince rejoiced to be in converse with his betrothed, be the topic what it might, and she was full of burning enthusiasm and all heedless of his growing passion.

As they talked they rode onward and crossed a wooden bridge to a flowered meadow beneath a crag.

"Oh, how sweet," he said, half oblivious, now, of the part he was playing, "to linger here with one who loved us!"

"Yes," she answered, "or with fair philosophers to elevate our fancies; for this, indeed, is a lovely place." Then turning to her maids, she called,—

"Pitch our pavilion here on the greensward and lay out the viands."

They raised a satin tent at her command, while she and the Prince set out to climb upon

the rocks. Behind them went Cyril with the
Lady Psyche and Florian with Melissa, and they
wound in and out the pathways of the cliff,
chattering geologic names and hammering away
pieces of stone, until the shadows slanted and
the heights shone out in rosy tints above them.

When the sun had set they came down from
the cliff, towards the plain below, where the tent,
lit from within, shone no bigger than a glow-
worm. Once, in the descent, the Lady Ida had
leaned on the Prince, and once or twice he held
her hand, and his heart beat with kindling pul-
sations at the contact. But when they had
reached the level and entered beneath the satin
roof, they sank upon the embroidered couches
in grateful ease. On a tripod in the midst rose
a fragrant flame, and spread before them were
fruits and viands and golden wines.

The Princess asked for some music, and one
of those beside her took the harp and sang.
When the girl had ended, the Princess looked
towards the Prince, and said,—

"Do you not know some song of your own
land to sing us?"

The Prince also sang, but a song he had
made himself, part long ago and part while he
sang. It was warm with a Northern lover's
wooing of a Southern maid, and when he had
done, all the ladies stared with wide-open eyes,

and laughed stealthily, wondering what to make of it, for his voice rang false and faltered now and then from the maiden-like treble he had assumed to his native bass.

The Princess smiled at the girl's uncouth melody, and chided her for singing a mere love-poem. Then she said,—

"But now to mingle pastime with profit, do you not know some song that gives the manners of your own countrywomen?"

And while the Prince was striving to remember some such ditty, Cyril, reckless with wine or in sheer bravado, struck up a tavern catch of flippant words about Moll and Meg. Florian looked imploringly at him. The Prince frowned, Psyche flushed and trembled, and the young Melissa hung her head in fright.

" Forbear!" cried the Lady Ida.

"Hold, sir!" said the Prince, and he struck him on the breast.

Cyril started up, and there rose a shriek among the women as if a city were being sacked.

Melissa called, " Fly for your lives!" and the Princess, " To horse! home! to horse!" And the whole troop, panic-stricken and bewildered, sped away into the dark.

Before the Prince could realize what he had lost, he stood alone with Florian in the deserted

pavilion, both cursing Cyril, and deeply vexed
at what had happened. Like parting hopes he
heard the hoofs crossing the bridge, and then
came another shriek, " The Head, **the** Head, the
Princess !" She **had** missed the plank in her
blind rage and rolled into the stream.

Out sprang **the** Prince, and saw **her white**
robe whirling in the waters towards **the fall.**
He gave **a** single glance, and **then,** clad in
woman's vestments as he was, plunged **into the**
flood and **caught** her. Oaring with **one arm**
and bearing her up with the other, he tried to
reach the shore, but it was in vain. **They** drove,
at last, on an uprooted tree that hung over the
water, and, grasping the boughs **of** this, the
Prince, supporting the Lady Ida, at last gained
the shore.

Her maidens were crowded **to** the verge **to**
take her from him, and they caught her **in their**
arms and cried, " She lives." Then **they bore**
her back into the tent, **but** so abashed **was the**
Prince by what **had** passed that he dared not
meet her eyes. He could not find his friends
now, and he therefore left **her his horse,** since
hers was lost, and pushed on alone to find the
door-way to the college gardens.

By blind instinct he finally came upon it, be-
tween its two great statues of Art and Science.
He climbed over the **top with a great effort,**

dropping on the grass within, and paced back
and forth in a tumult of thought, till at last a
light step echoed, and then a lofty female form
came into view through the uncertain gloom.
At first he thought it was Ida herself, but it
proved to be Florian.

"Hush," said he; "they are seeking us. 'Seize
the strangers!' is the cry everywhere. How
came you here?"

The Prince told him.

"I," said he, "came back with the rest, sus-
pected and avoided. I crept into the hall and
slipped behind a statue, and saw the girls called
up for trial. Each one disclaimed all knowledge
of us, until, last of all, came Melissa. I pitied
her, poor child. At first she was silent, but
when she was pressed closer she confessed; and
then, when they asked if her mother knew, or
Psyche, she refused to say. The Princess formed
her own conclusion and sent for Psyche, but she
could not be found. She called for Psyche's
child to cast it out-of-doors. Then she sent for
Blanche to accuse her face to face. I slipped
away and came here. But where will you go
now? And where are Psyche and Cyril? Both
have gone. What if they have gone together?
Would we had never come! I dread his wild-
ness and the travel through the dark."

"And yet," said the Prince, "you wrong him

more than **I did, who** struck him. His is not
the nature of the clown, to wrong what he loves.
For however wild he may be in frolic, as to-
night, **yet he has a true** heart **under his gayety."**

Scarcely had **the Prince done speaking when**
from a tamarisk near by sprang two Proctors,
crying, "Names!" Florian **standing** still was
taken, **but the** Prince escaped, **and led his pur-**
suer a race through all the windings **of the gar-**
den.   At last his foot caught in a vine, and he
tripped and clasped the feet of a statue, and
was caught and known at once.

They were taken immediately before the Prin-
cess, who sat **enthroned in the hall** with a single
lamp above her and handmaids on either side,
bowing towards **her** and combing out **her long**
hair, still damp **from the river.** Close behind
her were eight strong daughters of the plough,
huge women of the **open air,** ready to do her
commands.

As the captives were brought in, the crowd
divided, and they went upward **to the** throne.
There beside it lay Psyche's babe, half naked
as it had been snatched from bed.   At the left
Melissa knelt in tears, but the Lady Blanche
stood up and defended **herself in** vigorous
speech, rehearsing all her wrongs since Psyche
came into the college, and rating her own virtues
at no niggardly value.

To her the Princess coldly replied, " Good. But your oath is broken. We dismiss you. You can go at once. As for this lost lamb, we take it to ourself for redemption."

The Lady Blanche snarled out a defiance and caught Melissa by the arm to drag her away. The girl cast an imploring look on Ida, which touched Florian to the heart; and while all were gazing on her as she hung like a daughter of Niobe, one arm appealing to Heaven, a little stir began about the door-way, and on a sudden in rushed a post-woman, out of breath, who went straight to the throne, where she knelt and delivered despatches. The Head took them and tore them open in visible amazement. As she read, a wrathful flush spread over her cheeks and bosom, and her breath came half in sobs. The papers rustled in her trembling hand through the dead hush; then the babe at her feet began to cry; and this jarred on her anger. She crushed the scrolls together and made a sudden movement as if to speak, but utterance failed her, and she whirled the letters to the Prince as who should say, " Read."

One letter was from the King, her father:

" Fair daughter, when we sent the Prince to you we were not aware of your ungracious laws. We came after him in haste to hinder any wrong, but we fell into his father's hands, who has this night slipped **round** in the dark and invested you. He keeps me hostage for his son."

The other was from the Prince's father to **the Princess**, and ran :

" You have **our son!** Do not touch a hair of his head. Render him up unscathed and give **him** your hand forthwith. Keep your contract, or **we will** this very night destroy your palace."

Thus far the Prince read, then stood up and spoke impetuously,—

" Hear me, **O noble Ida,** and believe that **I** speak the truth. I and my companions came **hither** not **to** pry into your reserve, but led by golden hopes,—hopes that sprang from the royal compact made long ago. As a child I babbled of you. My nurse would tell me tales about your land to beguile me into rest. As a boy you stooped to me from all high places and lived in all fair lights. At morning and evening **I** heard the woods ring with your name, and you were a part of all I beheld on land or sea. **As I** would have striven to reach you had you been imprisoned in some other world, so, my youth past and manhood giving me the firmer will, I came and **found you here.** You were more than all I had dreamed or desired, more than the loveliest visions of boyhood, more than the serene ideals of thoughtful youth, and as I lingered near you through the days the beauty ripened and deepened to my senses, and I cannot leave you, O my Princess. I must follow you forever. And yet I did not come to you all unauthorized." And then on one knee he reached up to her her father's letter, and she caught it and dashed it unopened at her feet. A tide of fierce words seemed to falter at her lips just ready to burst, and she would have spoken, but there rose a great hubbub in the court below, where half the girls were gathered together in a noisy confusion crying out in fear of the rumored invasion.

The Head stood up, robed in her loose black hair, and moved to the open window. She stretched forth her arms and called out across the tumult, and at once it ceased.

" What do you fear ? Am I not your Head ? The storm breaks on me first of all. I am able to bear it; what, then, do you fear ? Peace ! our defenders will come. And if they do not come, what matter ? I will unfurl our banner and meet the foe, or die proudly the first martyr of our cause."

Hereupon the crowd dissolved and moved away, and the Lady Ida turned to the Prince with mock civilities and praise that had a bitterness beneath it. Then she burst forth into uncontrolled anger.

" I trample on your offers and on yourself !" she cried. " Begone, sir ! Your falsehood is hate-

ful to us. Here, push them from the gates."
And her stalwart attendants advanced mena-
cingly. Twice the Prince sought to plead his
cause; but the heavy hands were on his shoulder, and he and Florian were forced rudely from
her presence, and, amid grim jeers and laughter,
thrust out of the gates.

They crossed the road and gained a little
mound, from which they could see the lights
within and hear the murmur of the voices.

As the Prince listened he was seized once
again with his ghostly malady, and all the
past, Princess and monstrous women-guards,
the cataract and the warring Kings, were
shadows. This went by anon, as swiftly as it
came, but it left him under a cloud of melancholy, which shaking off as best he could, he
and Florian moved away into the darkness.

IV.

SCARCELY had the Prince and Florian gone
three paces when they were saluted by a sen-
tinel's voice:

"Stand! Who goes there?"

"Two from the palace," answered the Prince.

"The second two; they wait. Pass on," said
the voice.

Then a soldier in clanking steel led them
through the avenues of tents until they heard

the royal ensign flapping above the imperial head-quarters. The two fugitives entered, and the sudden light half blinded them, while all within began to titter and whisper together at their woman's garb, and finally broke forth into open laughter. From King to beardless captains the entire company shook with prolonged mirth, till at length the Prince's father panted to his royal hostage,—

"King, you are free. We kept you only as surety for our son,—if this, indeed, be our son— or art thou some bedraggled scullion?" for the Prince was drenched and torn with briers and all in rags. Then his father roared on, "Go, make yourself a man worthy to fight with men! Cyril has told us all."

Florian and the Prince stole away and changed their female attire for glittering armor, and came forth into the morning sun, which now had risen full above the northern hills. Here Cyril met them, at first a little shyly, but by and by they asked a mutual pardon, and then began the exchange of news. Cyril had fled away through the darkness, and later in the night had come upon the weeping Psyche. "Then we fell into the King's hands," he said, "and she lies over there still and speechless." He pointed to a tent a stone's throw away, and they went thither and entered.

Within, among piles of arms and accoutre-
ments, wrapped in a soldier's cloak, upon the
ground, lay Psyche; at her head a wrinkled
old woman, follower of the camp, was crouching like a watcher of the dead.

Then Florian knelt down by her and whispered, "Come, sweet sister, lift up your head.
You have done no wrong. You could not slay
me nor your Prince. Look up; be comforted."

The Prince likewise strove to soothe her.
"And I, too," he said, "have I not also lost her,
in whose least act there is a nameless charm?"

She seemed now to hear, and moaned feebly,
and then sat up and raised the cloak from her
pallid face.

"Her!" she said, "my friend,—parted from
her,—betrayer of her cause and my own! Where
shall I breathe?" Then she cried with a new
impulse, "Why did you break your faith? Oh,
base heart! What comfort for me? None,
none!"

"Yet, I pray," pleaded Cyril, "take comfort;
live, dear lady, for your child." At this she
fairly broke down, and sobbed piteously.

"Ah me! my child, my one sweet child! Ida
will hold her back, and she will die of neglect
or sicken with ill-usage. For every little fault
she will be blamed because she is mine. They
will beat her because she is mine. Oh, my

flower, my babe, my sweet Aglaïa! Ah, what might not that man deserve of me who should bring me my sweet Aglaïa?"

"Be comforted," said Cyril; "you shall have her."

She veiled her face once more, and sank back upon the ground and would not rise again.

But now a murmur ran through the camp, and the scouts came in with rumor of Prince Arac's arrival. The Prince and his friends left Psyche with the woman, and, going out, found the Kings in parley.

"Look you," said the Prince's father, "that the compact be strictly fulfilled! You have spoilt this girl: she laughs at you. She shall yield now—or war!"

Then King Gama turned to the Prince: "We fear you spent a stormy time with the Princess. Yet they say you still love her. Give us your mind: how say you, war or not?"

"Not war, sire, if possible," said the Prince. "I want her love. War would not bring me that; it would gain me only her scorn. She would hate me for it."

"Tut! you do not know these girls," his father roughly broke in. "Look you, sir! Man is a hunter, woman is the game. We hunt them just for the beauty of their skins, and they love us for it. Out! for shame, boy! There's no rose

half so dear to them as the man that does what
they dare not do. A soldier wins the coldest
heart among them. I won your mother so; and
a good wife, worth winning, she was. But this
firebrand,—no gentleness for her."

"True," said the Prince. "But, sire, wild na-
tures need wise curbs. Ida dares all that a
soldier might dare. I saw her last night when
she rose storming and cast down defiance to
all opponents. Believe me, sire, she would not
shun death,—not even the warrior's. And yet I
hold her a true woman. But you class them
all as one, and make no allowance for varying
types. Were we half as good and kind as
they are, much that Ida claims as her due
would never be questioned."

"Nay, nay, you speak but sense," said King
Gama. "We remember love ourself in our
sweet youth. You talk almost like Ida herself;
and *she* can talk. Yes, there's something in
what you say, and we esteem you for it." Then
turning to the King, "He seems a gracious and
gallant Prince. I would he had our daughter."
He spoke on indulgently of the invasion and of
his detention in the invader's camp, and lightly
excused his neighbor for the trespass because
of the provocation he had received. "But let
your Prince," at last he said, "ride with us to
our lines. Our royal word for it he comes

back safely. We will speak with Arac. His influence is more powerful than ours. Something may thus be done. And you also," he said to Cyril and Florian, "follow us, if you will."

He bade farewell then to the Prince's father, who growled an answer in his beard, which let just enough out to give them leave to go.

They rode forth across the fields beneath huge trees where the birds piped amorously, and touched by their songs the Prince was led to pour his own passion into the ear of King Gama, who promised help and made many a kindly answer to the Prince's warm words. But they soon came within sight of Prince Arac's forces, who were advancing in warlike squadrons to meet them. A cry of greeting to the King went up as he approached, and then the army halted amid a great clashing of arms and neighing of horses. The drums beat, and a horn blew out a long blast, and there rode out from the midst of the glittering ranks three huge warriors, the tallest and mightiest of whom was Arac. The Prince recognized him, because about his every motion there was a shadow of his sister Ida.

When the Prince beheld this martial sight his desire for peace turned to a stirring impulse for war; but the King drew close to his three huge **sons, and,** now pointing **this** way and now that, **told them** all that had happened. They smiled **as he spoke of the Prince's** disguise, and **the giant Arac burst into a roar of** laughter as **he rode up to him.**

"But how is this, **Prince? what does this** mean? **Our** land invaded, **our father taken captive,** and yet no war! I care not in **truth** whether **there be** war or not; **but then this** question of **your troth.** She's **honest at** heart, **believe me, but she flies** too **high,** she flies too **high. Sweet** enough **to** those she **loves,** though. **But I still stand on** her side. She made me swear it with solemn rites by candle-light. I swore **by** St. something, **I** forget **what,** but I swore, and **there's an end. She will not wed;** so waive your claim, **or,** else, war, with or without my father's consent."

The Prince hesitated, desiring to achieve his **purpose by** peaceful means, and **so** the likelier **gain his bride, but one of the** stalwart brothers **whispered audibly,—**

"**I thought as much: the woman's skirt hid a woman's heart.**"

This taunt was more than Cyril's impetuous nature could endure. He flung back some piercing and bitter **words, and the** Prince an**swered hotly,—**

"**Decide it here, then. We are three to** three."

"But only three to three?" said the third brother,—"no more, and in such a cause? Every soldier of us waits, hungry for honor. Why not have fifty on a side?"

"As you will," said the Prince. "But it must be solely for honor, since if we win we are no nearer to securing her than if we fail. She would not keep her compact the more readily."

"'Sdeath," said Arac, "but we will send her potent reasons for biding by the issue. Let our messenger go through, and you shall have her answer before we begin."

"Boys!" shrieked the old King in terror, but his appeal was in vain. No one regarded him.

The Prince, with Florian and Cyril, rode back to the camp, and found that his father had thrice sent a herald to Ida's gates to learn if she would acknowledge his claim. The first time there was no response. The next time he was warned away by an awful voice within. The third time the eight monstrous plough-women sallied forth and belabored him roundly. But when the Prince told the King that he was pledged to fight for his bride in tourney, he clashed the royal hands together with a cry, and vowed he would himself fight it out with the lads. But, overborne by wiser counsels, he yielded sullenly, while many a knight started up and swore to do combat for the Prince's claim while life lasted.

The field whereon the camp lay ran up to Ida's very palace-walls, above which rose polished columns and great bronzes of exalted women that overlooked the marble stairways within. Here, the whole morning long, the lists were hammered up, while heralds went to and fro with messages from the opposing hosts. At last Ida's answer came. It was written in a royal hand, which trembled here and there in spite of her resolution. The Prince kissed it and read it aloud to the King.

It told of Ida's ambitions and ideals, and how they had been thwarted by a troop of saucy boys, who stole in masked like her own maidens, blustering insolence and love, and making claims upon her because of some old compact which she herself had never set her hand to. She assented to the trial by martial combat, and urged her brother Arac to fight manfully, for he was in the right, but not to kill the Prince, because he had once risked his life for hers. Then, in a postscript written across the rest, she warned him against treason in his camp, and spoke of Psyche's child as her chiefest comfort in her own nest of traitors. She took it, she said, into her own bed for an hour that morning, and the tender little orphan hands

felt at her heart and charmed away the wrath
that burned there against the world.

This was all the letter said, and when he
had heard it the King muttered,—

"Stubborn, but yet fit to breed up warriors.
This Gama has lost all his power by lazy toler-
ance, and she has taken the helm. But she's
yet a colt; take her and break her, boy! Besides,
they say she's comely. Well, I like her none
the less for her hardihood. A lusty pair of
twins would cure her folly. The bearing of
children is the wisdom of a woman."

The Prince paid little heed to the hard old
King, but took his leave and pored over the letter line by line, but chiefly over the few words
which asked Arac to spare his life. He mused
again upon his morning in the wood, when the
leaves sung, "Follow, follow, thou shalt win."
And then he remembered the sorcerer's curse,
that one of his race should fall fighting shadows,
and like a flash his seizure was again upon him.
All things around him turned to shadow, and
he seemed to move in olden tilts doing battle
with ghosts.

When he had partly emerged from his waking dream it was noon, and the lists were ready.
He put on his armor with all haste, and entered
the arena with the rest. Fifty were there
opposed to fifty. Then the trumpet sounded

I.—*i*

twice at the barrier, and the combat began.
There was a storm of beating hoofs, and the
riders, front to front, dashed upon one another
with thunderous clang of steel and splintered
weapons. Yet to the Prince it all somehow
seemed only a dream he had dreamed. The steed
rose on his haunches; the lance shivered in the
iron hand; sparks flew from the smitten helmets,
and part of the noble company sat like rocks,
while part reeled and fell to the earth, only to
rise again with drawn swords and unconquer-
able prowess.

Arac, with the twin brothers by his side,
rained down a shower of mighty blows as here
and there he rode, lord of the lists. The whole
plain rang like a beaten anvil, so fierce and so
ceaseless were his strokes.

The Prince marvelled that such might should
spring from the loins of the King, dwarfish
Gama; and then, glancing aside, he saw the
palace front alive with fluttering scarfs and
groups of women perched in its marble niches;
but highest of all, standing like a statue among
the statues, he saw Ida watching them, with
Psyche's babe in her sternly folded arms. A
single band of gold was about her hair like a
saint's glory, but from her eyes shone an inexor-
able light, too cruel for saintship. He thought,
as he gazed an instant upon her,—

"Yet, for all that, she sees me fight. What if she saw me fall?"

With this he pressed among the thickest of the warfare and bore down a prince, and Cyril fighting by his side slew another. Then Arac, with a malignant grin upon his face, made at the Prince, and all gave way before him as he approached,—all but Florian, who, loving his royal friend better than his own right eye, thrust in between them. But Arac rode him down. Then Cyril, seeing this, pushed in against the Prince, wearing Psyche's color on his helmet. He was tough and supple and apt at arms, but Arac was stronger and tougher, and he threw him at one stroke of the lance.

Then the Prince spurred on and felt his veins stretch with a fierce heat. It was but a moment hand to hand. The Prince struck out and shouted. His blade glanced, and he grazed only a feather in Arac's plume. Then dream and truth flowed out together from his brain. Darkness closed around him, and he fell heavily, with jangling armor, down from his horse to the ground.

V.

AFTER the Prince's fall the fight grew more and more sullen and determined. The hardier knights of both sides held out the longest, and the battle between them was grimly earnest.

There **was no** faltering, no slightest recoil from **the doom which must await** them. Each fought for mastery, and the courage of **the** opposing sides was equal.

But at last **King Gama's knights** slowly gained the advantage, and **finally the day was** theirs. Then **there went** up a great cry,—

"The Prince **is** slain!"

His father heard this and ran frantically into the lists. He found his son, and unlaced his **casque and grovelled in** distress upon his body. **After him went Psyche,** but her sorrow for **Aglaïa** eclipsed her grief for the fallen Prince.

But Ida stood all this while on **the** palace **roof** with Psyche's young child in her arms, and sung a chant of victory. She was in an ecstasy of rejoicing **over the do**wnfall of her **foes,** and her tongue gave vent **to** sonorous words of triumph, which rang above all the murmur of the throngs below her.

"And now, O maids," she **cried,** "our sanctuary is violated, our laws are broken. Fear not to break them more in behoof of those who have **done battle for our rights. Come, since we are vindicated, let not our heroes lie uncared for in their tents,** but descend and proffer tender min**istries, that come** sweet from female hands."

With the babe still in her arms, she herself came down and burst open the great bronze

gates, and led a throng of maids, some cowled
and some bareheaded, as it chanced, into the
bloody lists. The Lady Blanche followed timidly
at a distance, but Ida entered undaunted, and
went straight to where her wounded brothers
lay. There she knelt on one knee, resting the
child upon the other, and pressed their hands
and called them her deliverers and a score more
of noble names.

"You shall not lie in the tents, but here in our
college," she murmured, lovingly, "and nursed
by those you fought for and served by all our
willing hands."

Then, whether impelled either by such soften-
ing contact, or likelier by chance, she moved towards the Prince. The old King rose from his
son's side as she approached, and glared at her
silently but with threatening aspect. But when
she saw the youthful figure lying dishelmed and
mute, without a motion, and cold even to her,
she drew a sigh; and as she raised her eyes to
the father's haggard face and beheld his beard,
grisly and reverend with age, all dabbled with
his own son's blood, she shuddered and her
mouth twitched with pain. At last she spoke,—

"O sire, he saved my life, and my brother
slew him for it."

She said no more than this; and the old King,
in utter scorn, drew forth from the boy's neck

the portrait of her and the tress of her hair
which he always wore there.

She saw these and recognized them; and a
day rose up out of the past into her memory
when her mother, the Queen, cut the tress with
many kisses, long, long before the time of Lady
Blanche and her formal theories. Then once
again she looked down at the Prince's pale face
and stark, immovable form. As by a flash of
light she seemed to recognize the bitter results,
the vain and heartless work wrought by errant
fancy and vague ideals. She was touched anew
to the sense of human needs and the blessings
of human fellowship.

She bowed her head and set the child upon
the ground, then she tenderly touched the
Prince's brow.

"O Sire," she suddenly cried, "touch him!
He lives; he is not dead. Come, let him be
brought here with my brothers into our own
palace. I will tend him like one of them. The
thanks I owe him win me from my goal!"

The King stooped anxiously over his son;
and Ida, from the opposite side, bent down,
and the two heads touched above him, mixing
their black and gray locks like the meeting of
evening and night.

Psyche, too, stole nearer and nearer, till the
babe, that lay by them unnoticed on the grass,

spied its mother and began to laugh and babble at her, and to stretch forth its innocent arms for a caress.

Psyche could not resist the sweet appeal. She stood a little way off the group and cried,—

"My child! mine, not yours! Give me my child, I say!" Then she ceased, all in a tremble, and with a face full of piteous pleading.

The near-by groups turned to look at her. Her cheek was wan with care and longing; her mantle was torn and awry; and her bodice had slipped its hooks and fell away from her throat; but she did not heed this · nor know it. She clamored on wildly again, till **Ida** heard, and, rising slowly from beside the Prince, she stood up silent and erect. Her glance encompassed the mother, the child, and the Prince. But as she gazed upon them, Cyril, all battered as he was, drew himself up on one knee and caught her robe to his lips. She looked down at the armed figure sidewise, insensibly or half in pity; but when she saw his face, the memory of his ribald song darkened her brow, and she arose above him to all her majestic height, tall as a shadow lengthened out upon the sand.

"O fair and terrible!" he said. "But Love and Nature, are not they stronger and more terrible? Your foot is on our necks, lady. You have conquered. What more would you

have? Give **her** the child!" He railed long
and boldly against her hardness, which shut out
love, and at last, "Or if you scorn," he said,
"to hand it to her yourself, or speak to one
who owns to the fault of tenderness, then give
it to me. *I* will give it to her!"

At first the Princess listened with haughty
disdain, but her humor changed as he spoke,
and at length she took **up** the child and called
it by a score of endearing names.

"Farewell," **she said to** it at last. "These men
are as unjust to us as they always were; and
we **two must part,** my little **one.** Yet I was
fain to think **thy cause** might be **one** with mine,
that I might be something to thee in the years
to come." Here she kissed **it, then,—**

"**All good** go **with thee!** Take it, sir," and
so laid the soft infant in Cyril's mailed hands.

He turned half round to Psyche as she sprang
to meet it with eyes that spoke untold thanks, and
she took it and mouthed it, and pressed it madly
**to her bosom, and then, afterwards, she grew
calm, and said in** supplicating tones **to Ida,—**

"**We two were friends.** I am going back to
my own land. I was not fit for the great things
you planned. Yet say one soft word to me and
let us **part forever."**

The Princess said nothing, but gazed raptly
upon the child.

" Ida! 'sdeath!" exclaimed Arac, " you blame
the men; but who is so hard upon woman as
woman? Come, a grace to me! I am your
warrior. We have fought your battle, now kiss
her; take her hand. See, she is weeping. I'd
sooner fight thrice over than see her weep."

Still Ida said nothing. But King Gama,
moved beyond his custom, cried,—

" I've heard there is iron in the blood, and
now I believe it. Not one word? Not a single
one? Where did you get this hard temper?
Not, I swear, from me. Not from your mother,
either, for she said you had a heart—I heard
her say it just as she died: 'Our Ida has a
heart, but see that some one be near her with
authority.' I brought you the Lady Blanche,
and what did it profit you? And, now, not a
word?" He chided her roundly for her whims
that had cost so much good life, for her ingrati-
tude to him who had yielded so greatly, for her
fickle liking, which could so easily give up a
bosom friend; and then, exasperated into unwonted energy,

" Out upon you, flint! You love no one;
neither me nor your brothers, nor any one but
your own wilful self."

But Ida made no reply to his wrathful outburst, nor spoke a word to Psyche. Her head
bent a little, and she stood as if a relaxing lan-

12*

guor had taken possession of all her limbs.
Across her mouth flitted now and then the
shadow of a smile.

But now the Prince's father broke forth in
mighty indignation :

"You, whom I thought a woman! There is
no woman in you. Not mercy for your accom-
plice! Then I would not trust my boy to your
treacherous hands.—Here," and he called his
own attendants, "take up the Prince and carry
him out to our tents."

He rose from beside the prostrate figure, and
every ear awaited the fury which should break
upon him from those man-scourging lips. But,
instead, Ida's whole face broke into genial
warmth, and through glittering tears she
looked fondly once again on her hopeless
friend.

"Come hither, Psyche," she cried; "embrace
me, quick, while the humor lasts. Be friends
again with one whose mind changes with the
hour. Ah, dear traitor, too-much-loved Psyche!
We kiss you here before these Kings in token
of all forgiveness. We love you none the less
that we dare not trust you." Then, turning to
the Prince's father, she said, beseechingly, "And
now, O sire, let me be his nurse. I will wait
upon him as upon my own brother, so deeply
do I feel my debt of gratitude. You and your

people shall have full access to him, and I will send our girls away till happier times. Help, father, brothers! Speak to the King, soften him even as I am softened to feel the touch of nature." She wept passionately then, but the King made no reply.

"Your brother, lady," said Cyril, turning to Psyche, "ask the Princess if you may tend on him, for he is wounded also."

"Why not?" said Ida, with a bitter smile. "Our laws are broken now: let him enter."

Then others among the girls asked permission for their wounded friends and kinsmen, and Ida gave a grieved and ironical assent.

"Yes, let it be; our laws are broken now. It is best so."

"But why hesitate, your Highness, to transgress laws which you did not make? 'Twas I who made these laws," said Lady Blanche. She turned an eye of scorn upon the faltering Head.

Ida affected to pay no heed to her stinging words, but cried, in despairing fervor,—

"Fling wide the doors! Bring all in, friend and foe; all shall be cared for in our palace and by ourselves." She turned to go, her whole face suffused with hot indignation.

But Arac went up to her with roughly soothing words, and her father, the King, strove to console her with his aged tenderness. The

Prince's father, also, at last gave her his hand, and they were reconciled by the side of the fallen Prince.

Then the wounded were lifted up and borne into the palace hall, amid the astonished whispers of the pupils and the rustle of their silken attire. Ida took her station at the farther end, her two tame leopards crouched at her feet; but in the centre of the great hall the common soldiers paused with wondering eyes, amazed by its magnificence, and by the throngs of girls in the gay college vestments. The girls, in turn, stared wide with wonder at the unaccustomed entry of men in their midst, and all was silent, save for the hum of surprise or the occasional jangle of some piece of armor.

Then through the hush the voice of the Princess sounded, giving orders for the bestowal of the maimed warriors; and they carried the Prince up the stairs and through long galleries to a fair chamber shut out from sound and intrusion. There they left him; and all the day through he could hear dull echoes from the ground without of the departing chariots which bore away the maidens. But enough of the worthiest of the pupils stayed behind to nurse the sick, and these with the great lords from either host beside the walls paced freely out and in at their will in mingled converse and kindly ministrations. Thus was the sanctuary violated and the palace turned into a hospital. At first all was confusion, but day by day order was restored, and everywhere the low voices of the girls and their tender hands cherished the wounded knights. They talked and sang and read and went to and fro all day long with friendly and soothing offices, distributing flowers or books, like creatures who were in their own true element.

But Ida was sad. She hated her weakness, and mourned that her old studies were no longer possible. She spoke seldom, but gazed alone for hours together, and brooded over the disastrous siege which had brought such swarms of men to her virgin threshold. Her hopes were thwarted, her mission was useless, and the whole world seemed darkened by her disaster.

From such profitless brooding at last she came down and took her post among the busy maidens, and found peace once more in work.

But the Prince lay unconscious for many days. He did not know whose hands were nursing him, nor did he heed the whispered talk that anxiously murmured across his pillow.

Psyche tended on Florian, and Melissa was much with her, for the Lady Blanche had gone away and left her daughter, willing that she should keep the favor of the court. Florian looked with all the longing of a convalescent for the daily appearance of the small, bright head between the parted silks of his couch, and he found her blush and smile a medicine in themselves. He rose up before long quite whole and well, and under Melissa's guidance learned to help those of his fellow-warriors who were still bedridden. What wonder, then, that two hearts so inclined to each other, and so employed, should close in love?

But though Blanche had sworn that after their night alone in the open fields Psyche must needs wed Cyril to keep her own good name, yet the match did not prosper. Cyril plied her with references to the babe restored by him, and wooed her valiantly; but she feared to incense the Head and would not yield. But one day Ida came upon them as Cyril pleaded his cause, and, though her face flushed a little, she passed on and said nothing; and from that time they tacitly understood each other, and were as satisfied as if the troth had been duly plighted.

Nor were these the only pairs who were caught in the amorous entanglement. Love seemed to hold high carnival in the sacred halls, and let fly his arrows at random among men and maids, until every marble niche was filled with a wooing couple.

King Gama and Ida's brothers did not cease

to press the Prince's claim, nor did his father, who was now fully reconciled to her, fail to use constant persuasion ; but she was still obdurate, notwithstanding that she often sat long by the Prince's bedside in her daily mission of healing. Sometimes, too, he even caught her hand in his wild delirium, and after gripping it hard, he would fling it off, and shriek, " You are not Ida !" Then he would clasp it once again, and call her lovingly his Ida, and heap caressing names upon her, though he really knew not that it was Ida whom he addressed.

She often dreaded, as she watched his wild gestures and listened to his raving, that he would lose his mind ; and the fear sometimes forced itself upon her, in spite of her assumed indifference, that he might even die. These feelings, ebbing and flowing day by day, broke gradually, but all unconsciously, the barriers of her grief and coldness ; and these, and the sights and sounds about her, the share in others' woe, the weary attendance, and glimpses of the happiness of new-found lovers, brought to her an unwonted tenderness and then an awakening love for him who lay at her side.

At last the Prince awoke sane and whole, but pitifully weak. It was in the evening, and he stared dismayed at the pictured walls, not realizing where he was. The figures looked to him like a hollow show of life; but so, likewise, did Ida, who sat by his bedside with her palms pressed close together and a dew of tears in her eyes. He moved, then sighed lightly. A touch came at his wrist, and a tear fell upon his hand; then he, too, wept for very languor and self-pity, and, with what strength he had, he fixed his eyes on her, and whispered,—

"If you be what I think you, only some sweet dream, would you could fulfil yourself and be that Ida whom I knew! I ask you nothing. Only, if you be a dream, Sweet Dream, be perfect. I shall die to-night. Stoop down, then, and seem to kiss me once before I die."

He could say no more, but lay like one in a trance. She turned and paused, and then stooped down and touched his lips with hers. The Prince gave a passionate cry, and caught her in his arms. He felt that his spirit had united with Ida's in that one brief kiss. Then he fell back, and she rose from his embrace glowing all over with noble shame. Her falser self had slipped from her like a discarded robe, and left what remained the lovelier for what had passed away. She rose, now, and glided forth without a single glance behind her, and the Prince sank back and slept unbrokenly, with happy dreams of love and the life that was to be.

DANTE GABRIEL ROSSETTI

ROSE MARY.

DANTE GABRIEL ROSSETTI.

ROSE MARY.

I.

"Come hither, Mary mine. Leave the garden-close now, and sit by me. The sun is sinking, and the stars are beginning to twinkle. Come, you shall read them once more in the beryl-stone."

Saying this, the aged dame, Rose Mary's mother, unbound her girdle and drew forth from the folds of her robe a sphere of transparent stone, shot through with shadows and touched with hovering rainbow tints. It was, in truth, a miniature world, reflecting in its glassy depths whatever of the great world about came within the circle of its radiance. But to one pure enough to see it showed more than this, for it held in its glowing circumference the unknown as well as the known; the whole future, as well as the passing hour.

For a thousand years, so went the tale, this globe of beryl had lain in the ocean with a treasure wrecked from a Thessalian bark. It had cost a human life to bring it back to earth, and thus sanctified it gained magical properties;

147

so that now, as Rose Mary's lady mother held it out to her, it had a wondrous light about it and shone very strangely through the thick and twilit leaves of the garden.

"Come," she repeated, "you may read the stars if you will, or follow your knight Sir James of Heronhaye as he rides to Holy Cross to-morrow."

At this name Rose Mary turned from her flowers and hurried into the chamber where her mother sat.

"May I see him truly, mother?" she said, and knelt at the lady's side with eager hands stretched out for the stone.

But her mother's face saddened as she put back her fair daughter's dark locks and looked caressingly into her face.

"Yes, truly, my child," she said. "He rides away to do penance before he takes you to the altar; but there is evil news to tell. Be strong now, and here is our help." And she pointed to the beryl where it lay in her lap.

"Now listen," she resumed. "On the road Sir James must take there is an ambush waiting to attack him; but he will go in spite of all danger, and will go alone. No one knows where the foe really lurks, but here in the beryl you may read all things."

Again Rose Mary reached for the stone; but her mother restrained her.

"No, not yet. Listen! All last night I made sacrifice and strove in prayer at the altar. The flame paled in the sunrise, and I performed every needful rite. Now, nothing is lacking but the eyes of a pure and innocent soul. Look, then, my Rose, and read his fate!"

"But, mother, if I should not see?"

"No, no; uncover your face, child. Love will teach you to see as you have always seen."

Rose Mary's cheeks grew deadly pale as her gray eyes sought the beryl-stone. She leaned over her mother's lap and passionately stretched her throat, sighing from her very soul, as she said, "I see!" Then they were both aware of a faint music in the chamber, but there was no time to think upon the marvel, though it deliciously lulled their straining senses.

The lady held the sphere upon her knee.

"Lean this way and speak low," she said, "and speak of nothing but what you see."

Rose Mary gazed upon the stone with fixed and staring eyes :

"I see a man with a great broom sweeping away the dust."

"Yes, that is always first. But now look well. What comes next?"

"I see two roads stretching away and parting in a waste country. Deep glens and tall ridges lie along their sides, and a hill walls in

13*

the valley. **One road** follows the brook, and
the other goes across the moor."

" Both go to Holy Cross, daughter. But
what **of the** valley road ? **He** must **go** that
way."

" **It runs past** me like the turning leaves **of a**
book."

" Look everywhere for **a spear.** They will
lie close till he approaches."

" The stream has spread out to a river, with
stiff blue reeds and bare banks."

" Is there any roof near to shelter a hidden
band ?"

" **Yes ;** on the farther bank there is **a** single
one, and a herdsman unyokes his team there in
the twilight."

" Keep watch by the water's edge ; some boat
may lurk there."

" One has just slid out from the winding shore,
but a peasant woman is at the oars and a child
is steering. But, there ! something sparkled——
No, it was only a lapwing."

Then Rose Mary, growing weary of the search
and succumbing to the intense strain of eye and
nerve, **drew** back and cried,—

" It is all in vain ! **I have** missed them, and
they will kill him, they will kill him !"

" **For dear love's sake speak low,**" said the
mother.

"My eyes are strained to the goal, but, oh, the voice within me!" cried Rose Mary, in lowered tones.

"Hush, sweet, hush. Be calm and search the stone," whispered the lady again.

"I see two old and broken floodgates," resumed Rose Mary. "Grasses wave along the weir, but the bridge still leads to the breakwater. And mother!" she almost shrieked in her dread, and clung close to her mother's knee, crouching low while her hair fell across her eyes, then she whispered, fearfully, "The spears are there!"

The lady stooped and cleared the locks from her daughter's face. "So much yet to see, and she has swooned," she wailed; then, smoothing the girl's fair brow, she lifted her up. "Look, look, sweet!" she pleaded. "An image comes but once to the beryl. Do you see the same place?"

Rose Mary wearily opened her eyes and gazed again into the stone.

"I see eight men," she languidly murmured. "The weir is covered with a wild growth, and they are hidden by the water-gate. They lie about as if they had a long while to stay. The chief's lance has a blazoned scroll. He seems some lord. I cannot trace the blazon. Yes, there, now—I can see the field of blue and the

spurs and merlins in pairs. It is the Warden
of Holycleugh."

"God be thanked!" said the mother. "We
know now. It is your good knight's mortal
enemy. Last Shrovetide, in the tourney, he
strove to take his life by treason, and now he
tries, again. So, my lord," she continued, bitterly,
" we know you now. You will watch till morning? June's a fair month, and the moon is
full. St. Judas send you a merry night at
Warisweir."

Then she bent low again over her daughter,
who had sunk across her knees.

" Now, sweet," she said, " only one more look
and you may lie soft in bed. We know what
perils are in the valley. Now look over the
hills and see if the road is free there."

Rose Mary reached up and pressed her cheek
against her mother's, and she almost smiled, but
said nothing. Then she turned again to the
shadowy glass.

"The broom again," she began. " I stand once
more where the roads part. The hill-side is
clear, but the river lies like a thread in the valley. The waste land runs by very swiftly, and
I see nothing but heath and sky. There's not a
break for a spear to hide in; nothing, nothing
to fear."

She gazed on intently for some time without

speaking, but again she began: "Over there rise the heights of Holycleugh. Where the road leads up to the castle there are seven wide and deep clefts. I can see into six, but the seventh is brimmed with mist. If there was anything there I could not see it."

"Little hope, my girl, for a helm to be hidden in the moorland mists. They melt with every wind."

"The road winds and winds," resumed Rose Mary, "and the great walls come nearer and nearer."

"Enough," said her mother, and she took the bending head to her bosom. "Rest, poor head," she lovingly murmured. "We are done now, and know all that is needed."

Then, as she wrapped the beryl-stone in her robe again, she looked fondly at it, and watched the flickering shadows course through its glassy depths as if it still pulsed with the vibrations of the spell.

As it slid into its silken case, a strange music drifted once more across the room and died away like a light laughter.

But Rose Mary had heard nothing of it. She lay in a deep slumber upon her mother's knee, who presently arose and lifted her tenderly into the chair, where she sank with a broken moan into heavy sleep.

Then her mother went out to bear the news to Sir James of Heronhaye and warn him of his danger.

Rose Mary slept **long and** soundly, **but at last** she raised her head and rose up bewildered. She **searched** her brain as for something that had vanished, and then clasped her brows, as a sudden burst of remembrance came upon her. She **knelt and lifted her eyes in awe,** and gave **a long, sweet sigh :**

"Thank God that I saw!"

But Rose Mary's mother, after she had spoken with the knight, climbed a secret stairway and knelt **at** a carven altar, where she laid, at last, the precious beryl. It was engraved with mystic characters in a dead tongue, which a priest of the Holy Sepulchre had interpreted to her lord, who had brought it home to her from the crusades as a curious gift.

As she turned away from the altar where it **reposed she murmured the words of its charm,** "None sees here but **the pure,**" and then, with **all a** mother's fondness in her voice, "And what **rose in Mary's** bower is purer than my own **sweet Rose Mary?"**

II.

The days passed slowly in Rose Mary's bower, for she was anxious to hear from her wandering knight. He had set out gravely enough on his holy errand, but he laughed a defiance at his enemies as he bade her adieu. Yet she was disquieted by his long absence, and feared the warning in the beryl might have been in vain.

On the third day, as she sat musing in her chamber, her mother came up to her and touched her with a caress which had so much of pity in it that she was startled to her feet.

"What has happened?" she cried. "Is he wounded? Is he here?" And she started towards the stair.

Her mother detained her and drew her down to the stone seat beside her.

"Oh, my Rose," said her mother, "what shall be done with the rose which Mary weeps on? what shall be done with the cankered flower?"

"Let it fall from the tree, mother, and wait for the night. Let it hide its shame before the new day comes." And the girl hid her fair face with passionate tears in her mother's lap.

The lady rose then and softly lifted her child to her side. With a supporting arm around her she led her drooping into the midst of the room.

"Come, my heart," she said; "it is time for us to go. This is the sad hour foretold in the troubled nights. Yet keep in good cheer, for you have a mate in your shame who will not leave you. There will be peace at last, if we love each other."

But the fair girl cried piteously upon her knight.

"'Twas for love alone," she said, " and the repentant heart has made bitter atonement. 'Tis only three days to wait, mother, and he returns to me. Where may I go till he brings me back a bride? for they will all know me for the thing I am."

Then the pent-up tears came welling from the lady's eyes, and both stood weeping together.

" Oh, daughter," she said amid her sobs, " how could you deceive me? Your heart held fast its secret and I knew nothing."

" And yet," said Rose Mary, " how came you to know, mother? Did the beryl read you my heart?"

" The beryl has no voice for me," her mother answered ; " but it told you a false tale, because none but the pure may read the truth."

Her hand lay close to Rose Mary's heart, and she could feel its sudden bound of fear.

" Mother!" she cried, " but still I saw."

" Yet why did you keep your heart hidden from me? for I told you that sin must cast out the spirits of grace from the stone. Oh, my Rose, it veils the truth to such as do not question with sinless hearts!"

Rose Mary sat like a stone and said not a word, though her mother tried to clasp her in a close embrace to avoid looking in her despairing eyes.

Then, with one great sob, the daughter asked, pleadingly, " Where is he ?"

" He is here," said the lady, with a trembling voice. " His horse came riderless this morning, and now he lies within."

Rose Mary gave a wild cry and fell into her mother's arms.

" The cloud on the hills by Holycleugh, daughter," she said,—" it was there they lurked, not in the vale : that was the beryl's deception. They brought him home from the hill-side to-day."

Rose Mary sprang up as if some mortal agony had shot through her. She shrieked once, and then, overcome, sank down to the ground. Her face lay pallid white on her dark hair, and she looked so far spent that her mother leaned down and listened at her heart. Then she wildly kissed her and called her name, but there was no response ; and she rose quickly, slid back a secret door in the wall, and ascended the stair within.

Above, where the altar was, a little fountain played, and she filled a flask with water and hurried back to Rose Mary, sprinkling her breast

14

and brow. There was not a trace of color in her cheeks, nor a perceptible breath from her lips, and yet something seemed to tell that life was still there.

" Ah !" sighed the lady, " the body does not die with the heart." And she wrung her hands and hid her face, wondering how she could ever meet again the poor girl's woful eyes. Then she began to think of calling help, and she remembered the priest who prayed there by the dead man's side. She rose and sped down all the winding stairs to the castle hall. As she passed the loopholes in the thick walls, she looked out upon the long-known valley and the familiar woods and brooks, but they seemed to her only like the threads of some broken dream.

The hall was full of the retainers of the castle when she entered. The women wept and the men were broodingly silent. As the lady crossed the rush-covered floor the throng fell back, murmuring, about the open door-ways. A strange shadow seemed to hang upon everything, for the slain knight lay there in the midst of the hall, on the ingle-bench.

A priest who had passed by Holycleugh early in the day had brought the tidings, and he had guided back to the place those who had brought the bier; but since the hour of his return he

had knelt in prayer by the knight's side. Word
had gone also to his own castle that Sir James
of Heronhaye was slain, and the spears would
doubtless gather soon to track down the foe;
but, for the time, all was mourning and silence.
As the lady's step came near, the priest looked up.

"Father," she said, "this surely is a grievous
thing; but my daughter,—she lies above in a
swoon. Go to the topmost chamber as you
mount the stairs. Let your words, not mine,
be the first she hears when she awakens. Go
quickly, and I will come in a little while."
Then she knelt on the hearth, motioning every
one away from the threshold, and gazed alone in
the dead man's face.

The fight for life had been desperate, for it
showed still in the clinched lips and hard-set
teeth; nor had the wrath quite passed away
from the bent brow and stern eyes. The blazoned coat was rent in the golden field across
his breast, and in his hand he yet held the hilt
of his shivered sword.

The lady seemed not to heed the body, but
spoke fondly to the departed soul. There was a
light of pity and love in her steadfast eyes that
seemed to render them capable of seeing the
invisible.

"By your death I have learnt of your sinful
deed, Sir James of Heronhaye. You have done

me and mine a great wrong, and God has sent you this doom for a lesson. It was ordained you were not to gain your shrift in life; but may death shrive your soul and purify you. Ah, I know how well you loved her!"

But before she pressed her lips to his brow, as she started to do, she saw a little packet half hid where his mail-coat was broken at the breast. It lay on his open bosom beneath the surcoat. A heavy clot hung round it, and a faintness came over her as she drew it away. The billet was steeped in the blood from his heart, and fast to it was glued an embroidered fragment of his blazon.

She gazed long on the thing with a pitying look. "Alas! alas! some pledge of dear Rose Mary's," she murmured.

Then she opened it carefully. The blood was stiff upon it, and it would scarcely come apart. She found only a folded paper, but around it was wound a long tress of golden hair.

As she turned the paper over, she dimly saw the dark face above in its swoon. It was as if a snake had crept near and stung her daughter to death. With a shaking hand she loosed the thread of bright hair, and then undid the folded paper; and that, too, trembled in her hold so that she could scarce read or understand its quivering lines.

"My heart's sweet lord," it said, "at Holy Cross, in eight days, I seek my shrift, and there I would meet you, if you will, on the like errand. At the same time my brother rides from Holy-cleugh and will be long absent. We can be safe then, and our love will be undisturbed. Until we meet I send you a tress for remembrance wound around these words; so, eight days hence, may our loves be twined together, is the wish of my lord's poor lady, Jocelind."

Rose Mary's mother read the missive twice over with a distraught and wandering mind. She could not realize its meaning. But at last it broke in upon her. Her head sunk low down upon her hands, and she cried, "Oh, God! the sister of the Warden of Holycleugh!"

She rose upright then, with a long moan, and stared in the dead Knight's face. Had it actually lived? She could scarce tell. It was a mask for the blackness of guilt.

She raised high up the golden tress of hair and struck the cold lips with it, then let it rest upon them.

"Here's gold to pay your way to Satan," she said, sternly. "Your treason has justly found its goal!"

She turned, half conscious of a voice that called her, and looked upward. On a row of fair and lofty columns a high court ran around the castle hall, and from there the priest spoke to her.

" I have looked for your child everywhere, but she cannot be found."

" Fear nothing," she replied ; " she is not far away. But come with me, and we will look for her."

She reached the stair and tottered upward.

" Death's face," she murmured to herself, " is hard to look upon, but, oh, Rose Mary, how shall I look into your living face?"

III.

Rose Mary lay for a long time unconscious in her chamber while her mother sought the priest below ; but at last she emerged from the swoon, and a dawn of light seemed to break upon her bewildered eyes. She looked around her, dazed at the sight of familiar things, and her lips were hard and dry. She remembered what had happened only as one remembers a vague and troubled dream ; but her mother's and her lover's names came to her lips, and she uttered them with a dread she could not explain.

Breathing heavily with the exertion, she got up from the floor and dragged herself to the secret panel, which still stood open as her mother had unconsciously left it. She went through the opening, then closed the door and stood in the dark upon the stone stairway. But her eyes were more at ease in the shadow, and she mounted without difficulty. She had never known of this secret stairway, but she was not greatly surprised at its existence, as all ways were alike strange to her now. Once she thought she heard her name called from some inner place, and she paused to listen, but could not tell where the sound came from. A faint ray of light fell down the dark stairway at her feet, and this guided her at last into the chamber where the altar was.

There was no change in her face as she leaned an instant against the open door-way and then passed on to the pillar within. The room had a dimly-lit dome, overhung by a veil, at the pole-points of which were symbols of the elements: air, water, fire, and earth. On the north side there was pictured a running fountain, at the south a red fruit-tree ; the eastern point had a lamp burning brightly, and to the west there was a crystal casket holding within it a cloud. The painted walls symbolized the ebb and flow of Time, who held in his hands the key of his hoards and his all-conquering wheel.

Rose Mary paid little heed to all this ; but she stepped forward presently with a weary face, and lifted the altar-veil aside. The altar was in the form of the coiling serpent which old lore has placed deep in the earth's heart awaiting the final Voice. An open book lay spread upon the altar, and some tapers burned about it. But between the sculptured wings of a strange beast Rose Mary saw the beryl-stone.

The dread sight of this talisman brought back to her all the woful past. The hours and minutes seemed to whirr by her in a deafening swarm, and in the tumult the forms of death and sorrow and shame trod near her. She saw them circle through the stone with mocking faces, and then the mystic lights faded, and once again she awakened into full consciousness with a pitiful cry.

She took three slow steps through the altar gate, and drew up her body straight and tall. The sinews of her arms stood forth in hardened lines, and her face was deadly white amid her dark hair. She was possessed with a passionate hatred of the thing which lay shining there before her.

A dinted helm and sword hung above the altar, for her father had won by their valiant use the magic gift which he had brought back from Palestine.

Rose Mary moved across and reached down her father's sword, but she never took her eyes from the beryl, and still gazing she spoke to it :

"O three times accurst, ye who inhabit this stone! Ye came in by the might of a great guilt, but a weak sinner's hand will drive you out to-day. A clear voice has told me this, and that I shall expire with you. Oh, may God save my parting soul!"

Then she drew a deep breath, and with tender words besought her lover to meet her when she had wrought them both forgiveness by the destruction of the fatal sphere. Her eyes grew soft as she spoke, and a smile half trembled on her lips; but the frown of hate came back as she glanced again at the beryl, and she swung aloft with two hands the heavy sword.

Then she took three backward steps.

"For your sake, love, and for God's!" she exclaimed, and the blade flashed and fell upon the beryl-stone and clove it to the heart.

A sound like thunder roared through the room as the deed was done, and the echoes reverberated far away in awful vibrations. But when all was still again, the beryl lay broken in two, the veil above was rent away from the dome, and the chamber was riven open to the sky.

Rose Mary lay on the ground, dead. But no trace of the convulsion had touched her beauty. She seemed to rest, rather, in a gracious sleep;

and over her head she still held fast the sword
with which she had triumphed.

Then a clear voice said in the room,—

" Behold the end!   Come thou to me for thy
bitter love's sake.   By a sweet path thou shalt
journey, and I will lead thee unto rest.   Thy sin
withheld me from the talisman, but thou hast
won thy way to my home who hast now cast
forth from it my foes."

WILLIAM MORRIS

THE LOVERS OF GUDRUN.

WILLIAM MORRIS.

THE LOVERS OF GUDRUN.

I.

On the gray slopes of a valley of Iceland
near the northern sea lay Bathstead, and across
seven miles of open land rose the spreading
roofs of Herdholt. There dwelt in these fair
halls two noble families that were friends, and
between their boundaries the broad valley was
paven with green pastures, where browsed many
herds of sheep and cattle, the possession of the
lords of either hall.

In Herdholt lived Olaf the Peacock, who took
to wife Thorgerd, and they had five sons, who
were lithe and of fair promise, and two daughters; and Bodli, called the son of Olaf's brother,
also dwelt with them.

But Bathstead was the home of Oswif, whose
wife, Thordis, bore to him five sons, stout and
lusty lads, but with little wisdom, and a sole
daughter, Gudrun by name, who grew by her
father's hearthside into the spring-time of a
perfect womanhood.

Now, one day as Gudrun sat among the spinning-women in her bower at Bathstead she heard the sound of hoofs drawing swiftly near, and started up to see who came.

"That must be Guest," she said, "for this is the day he tarries with us in Bathstead." And she went to the door and opened it, and stood between the posts looking down towards the distant sea. She saw below her on the slopes a throng of gay riders who approached at a canter, and she watched them eagerly with one slender hand curved for shade above her eyes.

That year Gudrun had just come to her full height. She was slim and of a girlish figure, yet she could never hope to be fairer. She had golden hair which reached nearly to her knee, and white hands and a smooth brow safe from the lightest touch of time. Her lips were crossed now and then by a smile which betokened a coming danger to men, and her eyes were bluer than gray, but very sweet in maidenly directness. She was clad in a lordly raiment made of rich stuffs from the South, and as she stood there in the door-way the rough world about her seemed by contrast to be but a rude heap cast up by the waves.

But the riders drew rein now before Oswif's hall. There were twelve in the company, and Gudrun stepped out across the grass to meet them.

" Welcome, Guest the Wise!" she said to
the leader, a white-haired and venerable man,
who wore a red suit." My father is away at
his fishing, but he bids me pray you not to
go by us, but bide here awhile. He says you
and he, in the hall, are two wise men together
who can talk cunningly about the ways of
mankind."

Guest laughed and leapt down from his
horse.

" Fair words from fair lips," said he, " and a
goodly place to rest at; but I must get on to
Thickwood to-night to see my kinsman Armod.
Yet, I'll stay an hour, and you and I will talk
awhile."

Then he took her hand, and she led him into
the hall, and all his fellow-riders got down from
their horses and followed them, with a great
clattering, through the porch; and once within,
they had a plentiful repast and much good wine.

But amid the noise of drinking-horns and the
boisterous laughter Gudrun spoke quietly to
Guest, and he smiled cheerfully at what she
told him. The old man's eyes grew grave
now and again, and Gudrun seemed as if she
scarcely knew what she was uttering. At last
Guest was about to reach out once more for his
tankard, but the words she spoke arrested the
movement, and he stopped with his hand half-

way to the cup. His gray eyes stared earnestly
at her, as if unseen things were revealed to him.
She waited, in trembling anxiety, to hear what
he should answer.

"And thou liest awake at night thinking of
these things?" he said, in a serious and tender
voice.

"Yes, father Guest; but of all my dreams four
only give me any dread. But there's enough
of dreams. Take your tankard and tell us
some merry tales; this is no time for grave
matters."

"Speak quickly," he said, "before my glimmer
of sight passes away."

Then she spoke swift words: "In my dream I
thought I stood by a stream-side wearing a coif
upon my head. On a sudden I thought how
foul that coif was, how ill it sat, and I took it
from my head and cast it into the water."

"Well, the second one," he said; "hurry and
tell me all."

"I stood by a great water, and on my arm
was a silver ring which much delighted me;
but it slipped from my arm unawares and fell
into the water."

"This is as great a thing as the last," said
Guest. "What next?"

"I was on the road near Bathstead, and had on
my arm a gold ring. I seemed to be falling, and

stretched my arms to steady myself, when the ring struck against a stone and broke in two, and out of the broken ends came drops of blood."

" A bad omen," said Guest. " Now what of the fourth ?"

" I dreamed I wore a helmet of gold on my head, and was proud of its beauty; but yet it was so heavy I could scarcely hold it. Then of a sudden, I know not what it was, but something unseen tore it from my brow and tossed it into the firth, and I mourned deeply, but my eyes were dry in spite of my heart."

Guest turned upon her with an old man's smile, looking keenly into her fair face, until she hid her eyes with her hands; but he saw a blush rise through the fingers, and he sighed as one in sorrow. Then he told her the meaning of her dreams. She would have, he said, a stirring life, but she would outlive all the wrong and love that might come to her, and survive alone when all else had parted from her. The ill-fitting coif was a mismated husband, whom she would shake off and be freed from. The silver ring was another husband, who would part from her and be lost in the firth, as was his emblem, the ring. The gold ring was a worthier man, her third husband, whose life would be taken by another; and the heavy helm was her last mate, who would be a great chief and hold the helm of terror over her, though she should love him always.

When he had ended, Gudrun drew her hands away from her face and sat by his side with fixed eyes and pale cheeks, as one who sees strange inward sights.

"Thank you, good father Guest," she said. "It is well; but may you not see awry through these far-off years?"

He answered nothing, but sat still with saddened looks. Then at last he rose.

"Wild words, wild words," he said. "But now it is time we were on our way." Then as she glanced full at him he saw a bright red spot on either cheek, and a firm set mouth keeping back her grief.

She entreated him to wait, for her father's sake; but she seemed scarcely to heed her own words, so distraught was she, and Guest answered that he must start at once to reach Thickwood before night. Then she led him listlessly from the hall, and he and his company rode away; but he turned before his fellows had raised the garth gate and watched her standing wistfully by the hall, her long shadow lying clear against its walls. Then when once outside he turned again, and shook his bridle-rein and cantered away.

Guest and his company had gone but a little

space when they beheld a man come towards
them, who, as they drew near, greeted Guest
with fair words, and said that Olaf Peacock
sent greeting and would welcome him and his
company to his hall.

" And well you know, goodman Guest, that
meat and drink are ever plentiful at Herdholt."

Guest laughed : " Well, be that as it may. Get
swiftly back and tell him I will come, but I
must not tarry, for to-night I am to be at
Thickwood."

Then the man turned and whipped his horse,
and Guest and his people rode on slowly by the
borders of the bay until they came to a dale,
where they saw the gilt roof-ridge of Olaf's
hall.

Presently out of the garth came a goodly
company of men, and then there passed a joyous greeting between Guest and Olaf, who rode,
followed by their trains of well-looking horse-
men, through the great hall gate.

Olaf led Guest from room to room about his
castle and showed him many marvels of curious
workmanship; the painted tales upon the walls
and the fine raiment in his carven chests. At
last he gave Guest a rich gift as he left the hall,
and rode on with him a little way to point out
to him his sons where they bathed by the shore.

When they had reached a low knoll overlooking the **Laxriver, Olaf cried out, "There!"** and pointed where a throng of youths sported in the water.

Guest looked off and **saw the tide playing on a sandy bar at the stream's mouth, and** the southwest wind brought up to **his ears the echo of their** joyous shouts.

"Goodman," he said, "thou art lucky to have **such a throng of sons, if they** do as well on **earth as in the water."**

"There is nothing **yet to tell of** their deeds," **said Olaf;** " but look ! now they see us."

One of the bathers rose waist-high and sent **up a** shrill call like **a sea-mew,** and **all** turned **landward,** beating **the water to foam** and **scrambling up the shore after their** clothes. **Then the riders, saving only Guest and Olaf, who** took a leisurely pace, rushed down the slope to meet the swimmers.

"Many of them, **then, are not** your sons ?" **said Guest.**

"No; sons of dale-dwellers near-by. But **Kiartan, my eldest, leads them all** in swimming."

"Tell me their names," said Guest.

Then Olaf showed him Hauskuld, his youngest **son, and** Haldor and Helgi and Steinthor, and **as this last one rose and** stepped aside he **pointed to two who sat on a** gray stone near the **stream. One was a** tall youth with golden hair,

who held a sword on his knees half drawn from
the sheath. The other sat on the grass in front
of him. He was slim, black-haired, and tall,
and looked smilingly into his companion's face
as if listening, while one of his hands lay on
the sword near the broad, gray blade.

"No need, friend, to ask about the others
after seeing these," said Guest, "for without a
word I know Kiartan, who draws the sword
out of the sheath, and, low down in the shade,
that is Bodli Thorleikson. But tell me about
that sword. Who bore it?"

Then Olaf laughed: "Some call it accursed.
Bodli bears it now, but it once belonged to
Geirmund, my daughter's husband. He married her without my wish, but his love soon
grew cold, and he left her, to roam abroad. He
would not leave the sword, but she helped herself to it, and in return—so the gossips say—got
the curse that goes with it."

Guest answered nothing, and seemed to brood
inwardly over some weighty matter; but Olaf
cried,—

"Wise friend, thou hast heard all the names.
How thinkest thou? Which shall do well in the
years to come?"

Guest did not turn his head, but spoke in a
meditating voice:

"Surely, goodman, you would be glad if
I.—*m*

Kiartan had more glory while he lived than
any other in the land."

Then, without a word, he raised his whip, his
horse started, and he rode swiftly away.   But
as he galloped onward he mournfully turned to
his son Thord and spoke of many things, while
the great tears rolled down his wrinkled cheeks
and over his white beard, for he saw the woes
that were to be for the houses of Olaf and
Oswif.

II.

TIME wore on, and a part of Guest's forecast
came true.   Attracted by her beauty, a youth
named Thorvald wooed Gudrun and won her for
his wife; but she found before long that the chain
of wedlock was a galling one.   She hoped daily
for a change which never came, and began to
look upon her husband with scorn and dislike.
Thorvald was a coarse man, rough and passionate by nature, and little used to wait patiently
for things to mend; and as Gudrun came each
morning into his presence with her melancholy
looks, rage and resentment took possession of
him.   Gudrun was secretly glad of this; but
her husband could not long endure the estrange-
ment, for he still loved her in his impetuous
way, and he grew more and more vexed with
her.

One day as they sat in the hall at dinner his

passion overcame him, and, rising suddenly from
his seat, he cast his half-filled cup on the floor.
Then he struck her on the face, and strode out
of the hushed and crowded chamber. He got
upon his horse, and, without a glance behind,
rode away furiously over hill and moor.

Those in the chamber turned anxious eyes on
Gudrun to see what she would do. For a little
while she sat silent, then she called them about
her, and spoke gayly of this and that, like one
freed from a weight of care.

But Thorvald came back again in a short
space, and she met him so changed that he
thought his hasty blow had brought better days.
She seemed happy enough as time passed, but
he misdoubted her humor, and gayly went his
way, keeping harsh thoughts aside.

In the spring he rode out one morning to the
court, not over-light of heart or free from fear,
though she parted from him kindly and frankly.
But the next day Gudrun went alone with one
man to Bathstead, and there told her tale; and,
as in that time the law did not hold tight those
who no longer loved, and as her kin were a mighty
folk, she received her divorce, and rode speedily
homeward.

Once more she dwelt at Bathstead, and was
wooed by Thord, who also won her love and
wedded her. He was a brave and fair-looking

man, and their life was a happy one, for she loved him truly. She put from before her eyes the strange things told her by Guest, and tried to forget them. But, forgotten or remembered, fate works out its will; and when they had lived together for three happy months, on a June night, as the southwest wind blew storm across Gudrun's sleeping head, her husband's body was tossed towards the cliffs by the angry firth. Rumor told that he was drowned by wizard spells in a summer gale.

So back went Gudrun to Bathstead again. She sat many a day with a fierce heart brooding over her pain, for life seemed made to torture her; and yet through all her woe the words of Guest would come constantly to her mind and quicken her into consoling thoughts.

The months wore on and spring arrived with its unspoken longings, and now Kiartan's name began to be heard on every man's tongue, for his deeds of prowess grew famous through the land. He was too noble to excite envy, and his fairness of face and limb was a wonder to look upon. He was leader in every game of strength and swiftness, he knew the craft of the smithy, and in speech he was most wise, and very gentle, so that all the little children loved him.

But while others praised Kiartan, Gudrun sat

apart, brooding on her lost days of happiness
and thinking how worthless such fame as Kiartan's was.

Then, when midsummer was drawing near,
one evening as the household sat in the hall,
they heard one voice call to another far away in
the valley, and afterwards the sound of approaching hoofs. Oswif rose and went into the porch,
and greeted the travellers as they arrived at his
threshold; but Gudrun sat alone on the high
dais when all were gone out into the porch,
and played unconsciously with her finger-rings,
musing on her one day-long theme.

Presently all the company began to come back
again, and she turned towards their voices in
spite of her melancholy. They brought lighted
torches in, and laughed loudly as they entered.
Then as the guests came down the long hall
she knew Olaf the Peacock, who was hand in
hand with her father. Behind them came two
young men, and she began against her will to
recall the tales told of Kiartan, because she
thought the one with the hair which shone gold
in the torch-gleam was he, and that the black-
haired and high-browed one must be Bodli.

By that time they came up to where she sat,
and she felt vexed that she must rise to welcome them. Then Olaf took her hand and
looked at her compassionately.

16

"Sweet Gudrun," he said, "I know your fate has been ill, but better days will surely come by and by. Believe me, not for nothing do eyes like yours shine upon the hard world. You will bless us yet, and all your woes will be forgotten."

She made no answer, but drew away her hand, and felt her grief grow deeper still that men should thus speak to her. But, turning around, she saw Kiartan gazing upon her with hungry eyes and parted lips. A strange joy entered her listless heart, and in an instant her old world was all changed. Before she could reflect on the cause, all her woe passed away, and her life grew sweet again, and she scarcely felt the ground beneath her feet. Her eyes were soft with tears that did not fall, and she reached out her hand to him. Her cheeks burned with the shame of love, and her lips quivered as if they longed to speak what they had never learned and might not utter till night and loneliness should teach it to her.

Kiartan's face beamed with a happy smile, and he was loving and confident, as he spoke in a voice which mingled music with might:

"They say your dead, lady, will never die, and I thought to have labor enough to draw you from the grave of the old days to-night; but you remember, I see, the days earlier yet,

when we came together as younglings. Surely
your eyes look kindly on me now, and it must
be because of this."

A brief shadow crossed Gudrun's face, but
she answered eagerly, "Ah, if only such pleasant days might last! What joy it was to wander
hand in hand gathering shells by the beach!"
She wondered at the sound of her own voice, so
strange an accent it had. She chid her heart
for rejoicing, and yet felt full of fear for some
unknown reason. But quickly every emotion
was stilled as Kiartan sat down beside her.

Old Oswif smiled to see her so changed, and
Olaf laughed outright for joy. Bodli sat by
them, full of pleasure in their newly kindled
liking; and the whole place ran over with merriment and good-will because of Gudrun's restoration to happiness.

At last in the glimmer of moonlight Olaf and
his company rode homeward, each with thoughts
which were born of the new hope: Kiartan
weaving dreams of the bliss to be, Bodli rejoicing in his foster-brother's good fortune, and
Olaf full of the glory which should spring from
these to perpetuate his noble line.

But Gudrun was sorely vexed by the conflict
of new and old thoughts. She watched Kiartan
go away, and her heart sank within her. The
wave of pity and shame flowed back upon her

and struggled with her growing love. Yet the very struggle strengthened her passion and made her yearn anew for its object, no matter . what seeds of ill might be hidden there. Then she fell asleep, and lay at rest beneath the in-looking moon, which fell across her tumbled bed and searched out her white breast and one arm buried deep in her wealth of hair. She seemed very beautiful and soft that night of her new birth into love and life.

Seven miles was but a little space to part two lovers such as these, and very soon the threshold of Bathstead hall echoed as often to Kiartan's step as to the sweep of Gudrun's silken hem. Life grew to them something sweeter than words could tell. To waken in the morning and watch from the casement the narrow winding way that led up to the hall; to feel the flutter of heart as memory gave place to rapturous sight at the threshold, these were dear experiences; and then the long hours of converse, when each word was like music which fell through the ear and clung to the heart; and, sweetest of all, the very minute of parting, because then Love lifted the veil and became a living thing, and showed himself palpably to them as their lips and hands drew back and they went from each other till the morrow. The long nights, too, held manifold joys of waking and sleeping dreams.

And yet through all her bliss Gudrun could
hear sometimes the strain of Guest's prophecy,
and her happy mind would darken at the in-
truding thought. But she put away the warning, and lived only in the present, and what she
herself refused to heed no other divined: so all
the country-side rejoiced that two such houses
were to be tied fast by wedlock, for the thing
portended long years of peace.

Now, Bodli was still overshadowed by the
fame of Kiartan, but he was second only to him
in all men's minds. Though he needed the love
of his fellows more than Kiartan did, yet he
was less able to move their hearts; but the
mutual trust and fellowship of the cousins were
undiminished, and Olaf loved his son scarcely
more than his nephew. Since Kiartan had begun to woo Gudrun, he and Bodli seemed drawn
closer together than ever before. In truth,
there was no concealment of thought or act
between them.

Thus as day by day Kiartan fared to Bathstead, he found the road always shorter if Bodli
rode by his side. He would pour his love for
Gudrun into his companion's willing ears and
ease his heart of its load of passion, while Bodli
in turn loved to mock him with light raillery
about Gudrun. Yet Kiartan saw covertly that
his brother's heart was kindling under the

influence of his own, though as yet it found no lodgement for its passion.

But one day as the three talked together they began to name over in sport all the fair and good women they knew who were yet unwedded, pretending so to choose Bodli a mate.

" Then over-sea," said Kiartan. " There may be one to suit over-sea. Go forth and win her!"

Bodli laughed, and cast upon the table his great sword with its iron hilt.

" Go, sword," he said, " and fetch me a bride. I will stay here in Iceland with those who love me. Go!"

Then Gudrun said, " Things more strange have happened than that we three should some day float upon the Thames or Seine. There's little to gain biding here at this cold end of the world."

Kiartan sprang up and threw his sword aloft and caught it by the hilt as it fell. " Would that the bark was at this very moment ready to bear us out!" he cried. " Oh, would that we could see Italy above the horizon there! But sheathe your sword, Bodli, till I give the word, and wait till you hear from me, Gudrun."

She looked lovingly at him, and Bodli saw her hand reach nearer and nearer to his. Then Bodli got up and sheathed his sword.

" No, if I am so hard to marry, I think I

must go a-roving. I will speak with Oswif and learn the truth about the warfare between Olaf Tryggvison and Hacon."

Then he laughed gayly and went swiftly from the hall, and found the old man, and did not come back again until the day waned and the hall began to fill with people. He thought that Kiartan sat strangely quiet, and he saw an unusual glow in Gudrun's eyes as she gazed on him, and a shadow rose in his heart that made him look upon the world as something less noble, but still there was an unknown pleasure within him. On the way home Kiartan was brooding and silent or spoke in words of light mockery; but as the days wore on there was little change to note, and Gudrun and he were still all in all to each other. But they talked oftener now of fair places beyond the sea, and sometimes a look half like a rebuke would cross Gudrun's face as Kiartan told over eagerly the marvels of those other lands. Bodli fell into deep musings as he heard the stories, and had strange dreams that he could not remember when he came back to common life.

So the seasons passed; but in the autumn the foster-brothers rode to Burgfirth, where there was a ship newly arrived in White-River. They had some talk with the seamen, and Kiartan invited the captain back to Herdholt as his guest.

He gladly went with him, and thus they learned tidings of the warrior Hacon, who had been slain. His son was exiled, and Norway lay in peace under the hand of Olaf Tryggvison. The captain was full of praises for this king. He was, he said, the noblest man who ever held the tiller or cast the spear; and to this Kiartan listened eagerly.

But when he went to Bathstead, Kiartan talked less than before of his yearning to see the outlands, and when Gudrun would ask him of the thing he would answer her evasively or lightly and change the subject with a kiss. He also spoke of her less to Bodli now, though his brother (because of her beauty, was the excuse he made to himself) was more anxious than ever to hear news of her. Bodli began to feel that the times were changing over-fast when Kiartan could deny answers to questions which in other days would have gained a loving and instant response.

Yule-tide came at last, and the neighbors from far and near went to one another's feasts, and, as the custom was, all Bathstead went to Herd-holt. The revelling was long and generous there, and Gudrun sat in the high seat by the goodwife, where she heard the new king's name echoed from mouth to mouth, and much talk from the wayfarers of the south lands. A sharp

pain went through her anxious heart as she beheld Kiartan lean forward on the board in silent
and rapt attention to the news. She watched
him for a long while with sad and hungry looks;
and all the time Bodli gazed at them with a
fading smile on his lips and with eyes growing
more and more troubled, until he hardly saw the
people about him.

But the Christmas-tide went by, and the year
drifted on towards the midsummer. One day
in his happiest mood Kiartan came to Bathstead,
bringing Bodli with him, who was strangely
silent and dull, which Gudrun noted, though she
talked even more gayly than was her wont. As
evening fell down along the valley, Kiartan
spoke softly to her.

" Let us make the most of our bliss, dearest,
for I must go away from you soon. In a day
or two you will hear our horns blow the Loath-
to-go, and I must put on my fighting gear."

" And am I to stay behind?" she said, turning
with surprise upon him. " Others may call me
what they will; you know me,—kind and long-
enduring. If I am with you, I care not how
the rough sea treats me. Come, let me share
the glory. I will go with you and take the fear
you cast aside."

She stood before him with meeting palms as
one in prayer, and she was pale and weary-look-

ing. Bodli paced up and down the hall with clanking sword and set brows, scarcely less pale than Gudrun. The waning sun shone through the narrow windows and fell in gold upon her breast and clasped hands. Kiartan stood gazing upon her with a wavering heart. Love of her and love of fame were in sore conflict within him. At last he cast his eyes on the pavement and knit his brow, as though he meant to say some bitter word. Gudrun's hands fell.

"No, no!" she cried impatiently, "I'll not ask you twice to take a good gift. I know my heart, and you do not. Farewell. Maybe the Skalds will tell of other great deeds than yours."

Her face was deadly pale as she brushed by Bodli, who stood aghast with open mouth and hands vainly stretched forth. Kiartan followed her a step or two, then stopped bewildered. But suddenly, like a changing wind, she turned back and came trembling to his side.

"Forgive me, forgive me!" she said, with streaming eyes. "Do not take my words as men's are taken. Oh, fair love, go, and let your fame run through the lands, for I know that what you win is all mine, as you are all mine at last."

She threw her arms about his neck, and Kiartan, touched with love and pity, made offer to give up the voyage; but she still bade him go, and not be beguiled by a woman's tears. A mist was in his eyes also as he pressed her fair head to his breast.

"My sweet," he said, "we shall keep tryst once again to say farewell before the ship sails; then, when I come back with honor won, how good it is to think of our rejoicing!"

She said some little words no pen can write, and laid her hands against his face, and amidst his kisses played lightly with his hair. Then, smiling through her tears, she went away, seeming wholly to forget that Bodli stood by them.

But before the day arrived when Kiartan meant to bid Gudrun farewell a long-desired change came in the weather. A northwest wind sprang up, and Kálf the captain urged them to set out while yet it lasted. There was a great bustle and hum of voices in the hall over-night, and the next morning at dawn Kiartan, with Bodli beside him, led from the gates ten strong and well-armed warriors. Kálf pointed his spear towards the south, and they followed him, and rode away amid shouted words of parting from the household, in the midst of whom stood Olaf, flushed with joy, and proud of the brave setting forth of his kin.

That night Kiartan and his company came to Burgfirth, where the ship lay anchored in White-River, and on the morrow they got on board and sped away with bellying sail and long sweeping oar.

III.

AFTER much time at sea, Kiartan and his men came to Drontheim in Norway, where now ruled Olaf Tryggvison, and they heard on every side praise of the King's might and fame, and how he had turned from the old faith of his land to worship a new God and demanded that all others should do likewise.

Now, Kiartan was of a haughty spirit, and had come forth from his own country to find adventure, and not to bow to another's rule. He spoke with his countrymen who were in Drontheim and brought them to resist the King's command, and when the King's messenger summoned them to show obedience he was sent back with a defiant answer, but Kiartan and his fellow-Icelanders put on their arms and went up to the council-chamber in menacing array.

When they came before the King they were commanded to accept the new faith or suffer death, whereupon swords were quickly drawn; loud cries echoed through the great hall. And the multitude, led by Kiartan and Bodli, fell into deadly combat. But the King had no wish to slay the new-comers even if he might, and planned to win his cause by peaceful means rather than by bloodshed.

"Hold!" he cried to his people. "You are too quickly stirred to wrath!" Then he made friendly overtures to Kiartan, whose noble and forgiving heart was touched to amity by his gentle words.

Thus was good will sealed between Kiartan and the King, and Kiartan grew great in his favor, and lived with him in the palace as his guest, till at last at Yule-tide he and his followers were led to the minster in white raiment and hallowed into the King's new faith. Then as time passed the gossips whispered that Kiartan was to wed Ingibiorg, the King's sister, for they were day-long together, and she was fair of face and of a gentle and graceful mien, and Kiartan found much pleasure in her company, though he never slackened in his troth to Gudrun.

But Bodli brooded day by day upon his home, and waited longingly for some news that should free the Icelanders from the King's hold, for he knew that unless the priests who had been sent to spread the faith in Iceland brought back favorable tidings, he and his friends would still be detained at Drontheim.

At last, one day, the good news came, and also came cheering word from Herdholt and Bath.

stead that all went well, and then in a little
space the ships lay by the quay pointed towards
Iceland, and Bodli, flushed and bright-eyed, went
to bid Kiartan farewell.

"Ah, Bodli, you are glad to go," he said.
"Why, this is the best face I have seen since we
left Burgfirth."

Bodli frowned. "You are as glad to stay,
perhaps, as I to go. What! do you think I plot
against you, then?"

"You are the strangest of men, Bodli," said
Kiartan, puzzled by his words. "Come now,
leave off riddles, and let us be as in the old
times. You are as true and loyal as the sword
at your side. Whatever may happen, I will
trust you always."

Then Bodli changed and besought him to forgive his dark looks, that came because he must
leave his friend behind. He promised to tell
all their kinsmen of Kiartan's good fortunes,
and to bear the news to Oswif as well.

"Tell Gudrun," said Kiartan, gazing steadily
on him, "all that you know of my honor and
happiness, and say we shall meet again."

Then they kissed and parted, and Bodli was
borne across the sea to Iceland with a deep and
secret passion consuming his heart.

IV.

Now, one day in the waning summer Oswif
and all his sons went forth to the west, and
Gudrun stood by the door to see them off. Then
when they had vanished behind the hill she
turned and gazed long and fondly towards Herdholt and the south. She mused sadly on the
passing year, and thought how her heart seemed
to harden with Kiartan's absence. She wondered, too, if he would think her strange when
he saw her again. Then, yearning to have him
once more by her side, she inwardly pleaded
with him to come back,—come back, and be as
of old.

For a while she looked quietly out upon the
road, until the wind seemed to bring her the
sounds of a galloping horse. She trembled between hope and fear as the sounds grew plainer
and seemed to come from the direction of Herdholt. At last she saw a spear rise against the
sky above the nearest hill, and next a gilded
helm. Then, joyfully, she saw a man in crimson
armor, who, when he gained the highest point,
drew rein and gazed on Bathstead spreading
beneath him there in the valley.

In an instant the rider saw her, and struck
spurs into his horse and rode swiftly to the
place where she stood. He leapt down, and

met her pale and troubled face with the appealing eyes of Bodli Thorleikson.

A dreadful fear arose in her mind. "How does
it fare with him, your kinsman?" she said.

He drew back with a sudden pang: "Fear not,
Gudrun, I bring fair news of him. He is well."

"Speak out," she said. "What more is there?
Is he at Herdholt? Will he come to-day?"

She turned away then with a bitter-sweet
pain; but he made a motion as if to reach his
hands out to hers, and his eyes besought her
for a single look of welcome.

He told her how he had left Kiartan in Norway praised of all men, and how her lover had
bid him say to her that he looked to see her
face again. "So God be good to me, these were
his words."

Hereupon she turned around in sudden anger,
bitterly accusing Kiartan.

Then Bodli said, "Well, I have done my part;
let others tell the rest." And he turned to go,
but lingered on.

"No, no, friend of my lover," she cried. "If
I speak ill words, pardon me, for my heart
aches with pent-up love."

She reached out her hand, and he turned and
took it, and his eyes swam with tears. It
seemed almost that his vain dreams had at last
come true, and that he was born again to a hap-

pier life. But she slowly withdrew her hand and
stepped back.

"Speak," she said. "I do not fear. When
will he come? Tell me the sweet words he gave
you for me. Tell me of all his deeds."

Bodli told her the true tidings, saving of Ingibiorg, and she listened, trembling.

"Good, very good," she said, when he had
ended. "Yet why does he tarry beyond the
sea?"

Bodli flushed red: "Oh, Gudrun, must you die
for one man's sake, you who are so heavenly?
How shall I tell you? You may live long, and
yet never see Kiartan come back hither."

She stood motionless. Bodli stretched out his
hand: "They lie who say I did the thing, who
say I wished for it. Oh, Gudrun, he sits day by
day with Ingibiorg as lovers do, and men babble
that soon he is to wed her and be made king,
and that Olaf and he will conquer Denmark and
England."

She said some words in a voice which sounded
like the wailing wind, then she passed by Bodli's
trembling hands without giving him a look, and,
blinded by the fire that burnt in his heart, he
turned and got into the saddle, and knew nothing until he drew rein by Herdholt porch.

Three days he sat in the hall in black despair,
till his people began to whisper and watch his
17*

going and coming with a great dread. But on the fourth day a messenger came from Gudrun, who bade him come to her at once, and he got up and rode madly to Bathstead hall.

A great pleasure came to his heart when he saw her slim figure move towards him down the dusky hall, but when he saw her face he was hopeless.

She asked him sorrowfully to tell her over again the news of Kiartan, and while he told all the bitter tidings, a passion now and again swept through her like the impulse of freedom though a dove caught in the meshes. She waited till the last word was spoken, then flung out her arms and wailed aloud. Bodli stood silent like one who meets for the first time in hell the woman he has ruined, the while her sobs calmed slowly down to silence. At last a smile full of her wonted courtesy crossed her lips.

"Oh, Bodli," she said, "how good you have been to me! But why, why does he stay from me?"

He pondered what to answer, but she took his hand in the familiar way of other days and led him to a seat and sat down beside him. Then, as she asked it, he told her once again all that had happened in Norway.

"But how may I know," she said, "that this is true?"

" Would God I were a liar !" he groaned. " Oh,
Gudrun, you will find it but too true." Then
he rose and went towards the door, heedless of
her voice behind him. But yet, when he had
ridden away and reached Herdholt, the time he
had passed with her seemed a very heaven to
him, and he longed to be near her again.

Thus between varying emotions he passed
many days, often meeting her among her kinsmen at Bathstead, and sometimes alone. There
was little rest for him night or day, and even
death itself seemed to promise no cure for his
malady.

Kiartan still sojourned in Norway, but sent
home no word of his doings, so that Gudrun at last ceased to speak of him, deeming him
lost to her forever. Then the gossips began to
babble of a match between her and Bodli, but
they marvelled greatly at it, and held it a
pity that one so fair should wed a man so
strange and sad. But yet the thing came to
pass after a while; and thus the seed sown by
evil hands sprang into being and bore its bitter
fruits.

V.

Now, Kiartan at Olaf Tryggvison's court began
to long for home and the sight of Gudrun ; and
at last, after much entreaty from the King to

tarry longer with him, he embarked for Iceland. **But the parting** from Ingibiorg pained him **deeply,** for she had grown **to love** him with **a** great passion.

Then Kiartan and his followers, guided **by** Kálf, the captain, crossed the sea, and one day landed at Burgfirth. There they raised their tents, as the wont was, and held a fair of **the** treasure brought in the ships.

Olaf and his sons were away from Herdholt **when** news of Kiartan's arrival reached **the** hall; but Thurid, his sister, and her husband **Gudmund, came, and** Kálf's **father** Asgeir, bringing Refna, his daughter, **with** a host **of** others.

As Kiartan **began to ask news of this and that** old acquaintance, Thurid approached him with an anxious face and drew him aside. **In** some amazement he went with her.

"Brother," she said, "**I** feared you might speak of Gudrun. **You did** not ask for her?"

Kiartan trembled. "**I** thought ill news would come of itself. Is she dead?"

"No," stammered Thurid; "she is well—and wedded!"

"Wedded! And the Peacock's house? I used to think them valorous and my father **a great man. And Bodli's sword—where was it?"**

He looked in her face, then turned and staggered wildly away from her.

"Oh, blind, blind, blind!" he wailed. "Oh, Gudrun, I am back with all the honor won you, and who shall hear the tale of my deeds? Oh, how shall I learn to hate you, Bodli, turned into a lie as you are?"

He had gone some paces blindly, and now Thurid called him, and he turned suddenly around. All the noises about him sounded as if a great change had taken place in the world. The far-away shouts of the shipmen, the murmur of the sea, and the bleat of ewes on the downs,—all these, and even his own name, and the grass and white strand and distant hills, seemed but as pictures in some dream, with their meaning lost.

"In this last minute the world is clean changed for me, sister," he said; "but yet I see that it will go on in spite of my pain. Come, then, I must meet my friends and face the life to be."

She smiled kindly upon him, and they went into the biggest tent, where there was a crowd busied over the gay wares. Kálf was kneeling by a bale of rich stuffs, and close by him sat Refna with her slim and dainty hand laid on an embroidered bag, and her fair head crowned with a rare coif.

As Kiartan entered she raised her deep gray

eyes to him and blushed blood-red, and he inwardly writhed with bitter anguish because of
this, and because the coif she wore was the
gift Ingibiorg had given him for Gudrun at
parting.

"Do not be angry," she said. "They have put •
this queen's gift on my head against my will."

"Surely it becomes you well," he answered,
evasively, "and whoever set it there did right.
He were a rich man indeed who owned both
the maiden and the coif."

"So great and famed, so fair and kind," murmured Refna. "Where shall any maid be found
to say no to such asking?"

Then he turned suddenly around, and, laughing wildly, said, with a scowl,—

"All women are alike to me,—all good, all a
blessing to this fair earth."

Silence fell on the group for a little space, but
anon he began to talk to one and another in his
old gentle way, and through the rest of the time
they stayed there he seemed unchanged, for so
his father thought when he greeted him at last
in Herdholt. But Gudrun's name was not
spoken, either in the tents by the ship or in
the hall.

VI.

KIARTAN found all things about his home as he had left them so long ago. There stood the hills, there Lax-River ran down to the sea; the thrall and serving-man came home from fold and hay-field, and Olaf's cheery voice called above the mead-horns. The fiddle-bow danced, the harp-strings twanged, and olden tales of love and wrong were told as of yore. But there was one change that had a deep meaning for the home-comer: Bodli's face was absent from the hall.

Many woful thoughts pressed upon Kiartan's mind as he brooded over his wrong, and bitterness grew within him day by day. Yet the other two were as much in need of pity at Bathstead.

Theirs had been a dismal wedding, where every tongue was checked lest some word should be uttered to wound another's feelings, or some name spoken that should kindle the smouldering indignation into open fire. The sons of Oswif were silent and fierce, and Olaf shrank back into his high seat and seemed aged and weary. His sons looked doubtfully at Bodli, and more than once the hot words they would have flung at him were checked by their father's warning eye.

Then on the morrow Gudrun and Bodli began
a life void of happiness, but full of capricious
changes in mood and act. The hall which once
rang with gay and free mirth became silent and
dull.

But one autumn evening as Bodli and Gudrun, with her brother Ospak, sat on the dais,
there came to the gate-way two wandering
churls who asked for shelter. As none was ever
turned away from Oswif's door unheeded, they
were soon seated amid the boisterous house-
carles, revelling in mirth and ease. They
pleased their audience with coarse jokes and
themselves laughed loudest of all the table-full.

Ospak sat awhile in his place looking across
at Bodli with scorn, for he had grown to hate
the brooding looks always bent downward in
despair. At last he yawned with either hand
stretched out, and cried aloud to the merry
company at the lower table,—

" Well fare you, fellows ! What gives you so
much merriment ? We are not merry here."

One stepped forth. " Sooth, Ospak," he said,
"our talk's of little worth. These wandering
churls are full of meat and drink and make a
deal of fun."

" Bring them here," said Ospak; "they may
help to divert us."

The wanderers came up from the lower end

of the hall, ill clad and unkempt, yet with merry faces enough. They were a little timorous in such presence, but drink emboldened them before long.

"Well, fellows," said Ospak, "what tidings are afield? Where do you come from?"

The first man turned his leering eyes on Bodli, and a cunning grin came upon his face; but just as he began, the other, drunker and perhaps, therefore, wiser, screwed up his eyes, and said,—

"Say-all-you-know goes with a clouted head."

"Say-naught-at-all gets beaten," said Ospak, "if he has his belly full of meat and makes no answer."

"Do not be angry, son of Oswif," said the first; "yet Mistress Gudrun there——"

"Tush!" said the second, "thou art mighty full of fear for a man full of drink. Let her say that we shall go as we came, and all is soon told."

Ospak laughed, and, sprawling over the laden board, he sat with his cheek close to his cup. But Gudrun turned to him pale and with a great agony of hope striving in her.

"Tell me the tale, and have a gift for it," she said. "My finger is no better for this gold. Draw it off." And she reached her hand out to the man, who stood wondering at her, half sobered by her face and not daring to touch the ring.

18

"We came from Burgfirth," at last he said, "where about a new-anchored ship they held a sale. The skipper was Kálf Asgeirson, and many others were there."

Ospak still sat chuckling to himself and lolling over his cup, but Bodli rose up and began to pace to and fro, as he had done once before in that same place.

The man went on: "I saw Gudmund, and Thurid, and Asgeir and his daughter, as they stood about a man whose mantle was red as blood and fine as a king's raiment."

Ospak hereupon put up his left hand to his ear, as one who listens intently, and smiled all the while. Then, amid unbroken silence, the wanderer said,—

"I had never seen this tall man before. He carried a wondrous weapon in his sword-belt all gemmed and overwrought with gold. I dared not ask his name, yet surely, mistress, I deemed him to be Kiartan Olafson."

He looked around as he finished, as if he feared something would happen, but those three hearts were stirred no further by a name each expected to hear spoken. Bodli still paced the floor; Ospak beat a tune upon the board with his hand; and, saying not a syllable, Gudrun drew the ring from her finger and gave it to the news-bearer. But Ospak knew that the trinket had been Bodli's first gift to his sister when they had plighted troth.

Then the travelling churls went slowly down the hall, but one looked over his shoulder as he withdrew, and saw Ospak lean over to Gudrun and nod his head at Bodli, meanwhile pointing a mocking finger at his own breast. But Gudrun did not heed him; for she had but one thought: that Kiartan had come back and she should see him once again.

Night came slowly down upon the dull hall, and all went off to bed save Bodli, who sat alone in the high seat. It was nearly dawn when he heard behind him a light footfall. He did not dare to look around, till presently the figure was close beside him, white in the half-dusk of the morning. He tried to cry out, but his tongue clove to his mouth, and he had no power to reach his sword-hilt. It seemed as if his guilt and sorrow stood there bodily before him, yet when a dreadful voice spoke he knew it was Gudrun's.

"I came again," she said, "because I lay awake and thought about what men have told of traitors, and I wanted to see how one would look to me. Night, nor death either, shall hide you from what you have wrought, O Bodli Thorleikson! My curse upon you!" And she broke into wild gestures and an endless stream of bitter words.

Bodli helplessly stretched out his hands for peace, and said in a low voice, " Would God I were dead! and yet I hope to have kinder words than these from Kiartan before I die."

" Yes, he is kind, he is kind," she exclaimed. " He loves all, and casts his kindness wide as God. He loves me as God loves his crawling creatures; and who knows how I love him?— how I hate a face he looks kindly on? God help me, I am talking of my love to you, and I yet may prove even such a traitor as you before the tale is done!"

She went away then, but lingered close by, as if to hear what he might say. But dawn came up apace, the sparrows woke about the eaves, the swan trumpeted from far away, and the cold morning wind running along the hangings caught her unbound hair, drove her night-clothes around her body, and stirred the rushes on which she stood.

Their eyes met a moment in a strange look, and he rose with haggard face and trembling limbs as if to embrace her, but she tossed her arms wildly over her head and with one dreadful glance fled away.

VII.

THE days wore on, and Kiartan was silent about the two who had wronged him. But Olaf was anxious, and feared that some day his

son's smouldering resentment might burst forth
into a blaze of revenge.

Kálf the captain came often to the Peacock's
stead during that autumn and brought his sister
Refna.   At last it began to be whispered that
she would make a seemly wife for Kiartan, if
he ever chose to marry.   Refna heard these
rumors and grew full of foolish hopes.   But
Kiartan paid little heed to her, though he noted
well how she looked on him, and he could not
pass her by without seeing how fair and gentle
she was.

As Yule-tide came round again Oswif bade
the Bathstead folk to Herdholt, and all made
ready to go save Kiartan, who wandered aim-
lessly among the busy groups on the morning
of parting, but said not a word to any soul.

When Olaf heard of this he came to Kiartan
with an anxious face.

"Why will you still harbor wrath, my son?
Come, let the past be past.   You are young, and
may gain many another honor and love."

Kiartan turned slowly and said, with a sneer,
"Truly, sir, love abounds in this kind world.
One more than I deemed of loved my love, and
there's the trouble."   But as he looked at his
father's gray locks and wrinkled brow, he asked
more kindly, "What would you have me do,
father?   I sit here quietly and let others live

their lives as they will. Would you desire to wake up strife?"

Olaf denied that he did, but spoke his sorrow for his son's grief and loneliness, and plead with him to go to Bathstead with the rest.

So Kiartan at last consented, and once again he saw the place which of old had seemed holy to him. He made no outcry as he greeted Bodli, who came towards him with a shamefaced mien, but simply said,—

"Be merry, Bodli; you are nobly wedded. You had the toil, and now the reward is yours."

Then he saw Gudrun far away in the hall, and caught her gray eyes as they turned to his, and the three that were friends stood gazing at one another in silent bitterness.

The feast was spread, and the Yule-tide merriment went round the board, but Kiartan sat coldly through it all, watching Gudrun, still in her perfect loveliness, untouched by passion. Bodli glanced from one to the other in feverish dread, striving to pierce the masks they wore, and fearing each moment to hear a shriek from the broken heart of his wife.

When the day was over, Bodli brought Kiartan three handsome horses, such as had never before been seen in Iceland. He entreated him to take them, but Kiartan only said in a low voice,—

"Do not strive with fate, Bodli. You have
made your choice; gifts and love will scarcely
heal a wound like mine. God keep us wide
apart."

Then Olaf and his household went homeward;
and, as they rode together, Olaf blamed his son
for refusing the gifts, and plead with him to go
again to Bathstead. Kiartan answered duti-
fully, but he warned Olaf that the seed he was
sowing would one day bring forth a dreadful
fruit.

Now, it happened that through the tender
offices of Thurid, and because Kiartan felt his
heart touched by Refna's beauty, he came to
love her in a pitying fashion because she grew
pale in loving him, and at last he married
her.

Then the months passed, and autumn came
again, and, as was the yearly custom, the Bathstead kindred went over in turn to Herdholt;
and though Kiartan was loath to face them,
yet his father prayed him to put by his doubts,
and once more he was obliged to see Gudrun
and Bodli together.

Refna beheld Gudrun's great beauty with
troubled thoughts; and Kiartan noting this,
and how Gudrun sat in the hall as if she were
its mistress, grew angered. Then, as the guests
were marshalled to their seats, and the serving-

maid asked him who should fill the high seat beside the goodwife, he roared out, "Who, damsel, but my wife?" As he spoke he glanced at Gudrun, and their eyes met. She changed color, and he grew warmer still, berating the girl in scornful words levelled at Gudrun.

"You'll have to fight for Gudrun yet," laughed Ospak to Bodli in a whisper all could hear; and thus the feast began.

The next day Thorgerd called Refna to her, and bade her put on the rich coif given to Kiartan by Queen Ingibiorg. Refna reddened and looked with appealing eyes to her husband, who was deep in thought and said nothing. She went then, seeing there was no escape, and put on the glittering head-dress, and came to her seat on the dais looking like a brilliant star through the shadowed hall.

Ospak saw Gudrun turn pale at this, and he showed his teeth like a sulky hound, muttering that the coif had been stolen from his sister; but Kiartan went over and sat by his wife, and whispered that he liked her better with no ornament at all upon her fair brow. "Look down there," he said, "at Oswif's scowling sons! The coif may draw their swords upon us before we part."

Gudrun watched them, sick-hearted and full of malice, as she saw how Kiartan's hand lay on

Refna's and how close their cheeks came together. She was ready now to second her
brothers in their growing hatred.

Then the next morning, after the guests had
departed, Kiartan went to find his sword, the
gift of the King, which he had laid aside while
he bade them Godspeed; but he found it gone
from its place above his bed. He questioned all
his people, but none had seen it.

Meanwhile, An the Black, a sturdy house-
carle, slipped out, and came back presently,
panting sorely, but smiling all the while. He
carried something wrapped in his cloak.

"Well," said Olaf, "what has happened
now?"

An told how he had followed Olaf and his
party, knowing what thieves they were,—this he
said with a dangerous sparkle of the eyes,—and
at the Peat Moss he saw young Thorolf lag
behind and take something from his cloak. He
thrust it down into the bog, then swiftly rode
on again. But An came up to the place when
they were out of sight and drew forth the
sword. The scabbard was gone past recovery,
rich and beautiful as it was.

Hereupon he drew the bright and naked
"King's Gift," as it was called, from his cloak,
and Olaf was rejoiced that it was found, and
praised An for his achievement.

Kiartan spoke musingly, taking the sword in his hand. "Who can tell," he said, "but this, after all, will end the troublous tale? Well, I did not cast the sheath away."

VIII.

Now, although Olaf bade An hold his peace, and although Kiartan likewise promised to be fair-spoken to the kin of Bathstead, yet before long the story of the stolen sword came to be known far and wide. News reached Kiartan's ears that Oswif's sons deemed that they had cast a shame on Herdholt by the theft, and that they openly mocked him as "Mire-Blade." But Kiartan was unmoved by these rumors, and until the return of Yule-tide, when the men of Herdholt made ready to ride to Bathstead, nothing happened to mar the outward amity of the two houses.

When Olaf's household was ready to set out, Thorgerd told Refna she must again wear the queen's coif and look like the bride she was. Refna dared not refuse, but she entreated the goodwife to spare her, and pleaded that it might remain in her chest.

"No, no!" said Kiartan. "If it were only for you and me, sweet, there it might rest; but I remember how when I was a child and wanted some glittering thing, an axe or a knife, my

mother would let me have it, knowing that I
would be sure to cut myself in punishment."

Refna looked down puzzled and shamefaced.
Thorgerd turned to Kiartan with a frown, but
he only smiled and said, " Yes, mother, let the
gold burn among the Bathstead lights. Come,
we must play our parts openly."

So the coif was brought, and the company
once more rode to Olaf's hall and feasted as
merrily as was their custom. But when the
season of revelling was over, and Refna looked
for her golden head-gear, it was gone and could
not be found. She passed through the crowd
and whispered the news to Kiartan. Ospak
stood near them and bit his lips, watching
eagerly what they did.

" Well, let it be," said Kiartan ; " light won,
light gone. If it's still above ground, Refna,
doubt not it will one day be recovered."

Each one in the hall looked alarmed at his
neighbor. Thorgerd turned to Gudrun and
said, firmly,—

" I have seen the day when the kin of Egil
would kill a man or two for a thing of less
worth than this."

Gudrun calmly met her frown. " Was the
thing his own ?" she asked. " It is small loss for
her to sit without his old love's coif upon her
head."

Before Thorgerd could answer, Kiartan cried **out** to Bodli, "Come, ride with me to the hill by the beach. I must speak, cousin, what has troubled my mind these last **days of our** meeting."

Bodli flushed red, and, **taking his sword** from **his side, gave it to his wife.**

"**One sword will be enough** between us to-day," he **murmured; then, as they** rode away, **Kiartan** leaned **toward** Ospak and mockingly said, "**I love you. I would** not have **you die. Do not see me too often, because I have a plague sometimes that brings those who** come **near me to the grave.**"

Ospak's **hand fell on his sword-hilt and he shrank back to the doorway.** Kiartan laughed **gayly** as he and **Bodli rode jingling down to the sea.**

But the laughter passed from Kiartan's lips when he and Bodli **at last came to be alone.**

"You see, Bodli," he said, "how we two must **swim down this strange stream.** You are **weaponless to-day, and my** sword stays in its **scabbard. How long is it to last?**"

"**Until I am no more,**" said Bodli. "Shall I take life and **love both from you, Kiartan?**"

"No," he answered, "but you cannot be so sure **of it, Bodli.** Remember where you **stand, between a passionate woman's heart and the envy** of a dangerous fool. You are helpless. As a thing begins, so it must end. Ah, brother, the old days are still dear to me, in spite of all that has come to pass; but to-day I part from you and them forever. What say you, then: shall the days to come be forgiven? Shall it not be remembered less that we have parted, than that we once loved each other dearly well?"

Bodli gazed silently into his brother's face. "O Kiartan, why do you speak thus?" he said at last. "I do the wrong twice over in hearing you say the words."

Then, when he had done, Bodli started back, and the murmuring sea seemed to tell, from far off, of rest from pain. On a little knoll he turned about, and, looking toward the hill, saw Kiartan's spear glittering above its brow, but the warrior himself was hidden below. Then Bodli slowly rode home to await the end of all.

IX.

Now, one day in the spring-time Refna wandered by a brook near to Herdholt, and at last lay down in a grassy place and fell asleep. When she awoke she could hear the sound of voices near by, though the speakers were concealed from her by the thick leafage under which she rested. There were two women talking as they washed the household linen, and their news was of Kiartan.

"They say," one repeated to the other, "that though it is latter spring, yet Kiartan has done nothing to punish the two thefts of the Bathstead men."

"Fool!" said the second, "must he stir up strife for every trifle?"

"Well, at all events," quoth the first, "none of Kiartan's kin would have dared to do the thing to Gudrun. Listen, this is the truth, for every one knows it. Gudrun and Kiartan would be very glad were Bodli and Refna out of the way!"

Refna came to her husband with this gossip and opened her aching heart to him; but he only showered kisses on her and drew her to his breast. Her faith and love for him touched him deeply, so pure and changeless was she; yet he could not but think, even while she lay against his heart, of the hopes of old, now fallen all to nothingness.

For a day or two after this he went about with a brooding face, but at last, one noon, he bade his men see to their war array, and commanded that two hours after midnight all of them should await his coming in the hall. They were punctually present when he entered, clad in his fairest armor; and Refna, who watched the spears and glittering mail through the hangings, heard the rough laughter of the men and saw the red lights glare in the gray dawn with a wild alarm.

Kiartan found her before he set out, and gayly promised her a noble gift when he should return. "Do your part to receive it graciously, Refna," he said; "gather the fiddlers and glee-men here to make merry with you."

Refna guessed the cause of this warlike sally, and she grew faint at heart to think that words of hers should have led to it. She clung to Kiartan, but he gently drew her hold from his mail-rings and kissed her lovingly. Then she fell back in tears upon her bed, and presently heard his cheerful cry: "To Bathstead, ho!" and the noisy crowd clashed through the hall and passed out at the gates. After this, all was still, save the loitering footsteps of some maid getting back to bed, and she lay alone in great dread and grief.

But at Bathstead, before the household was up that morning, there was heard the far-away winding of a horn; and when they ran to the door, Oswif's sons saw a great company beset-ting every exit of their home. The Bathstead men hurriedly put on their arms and went out; but there was a tent of gay stripes raised on the slope against the hall, and Olaf's sons stood all around it with sixty followers.

One man, taller than the rest, stood some yards nearer **the** hall door, leaning **on** a pennoned spear, and clad in glittering mail. **He** had a shield about his neck bearing a picture of **the** Holy Rood, and out of **his** helmet fell long yellow locks. His eyes were hidden **by the brim,** but Oswif and his **sons** knew that it was **Kiartan, and a great fear** overtook them, notwithstanding their fiery hatred of him and his kin.

Ospak alone among his fellows did not quail, **but** strode **out** before the rest, crying,—

"**We were wont to receive you inside,** not **out, Kiartan Olafson.** What have you done, that you are forbidden **to enter?**"

The tall man **did not move, but a deep voice came from the helm,**—

"I am sick now, and somewhat deadly to those **who come** near me. My sword has lost its scabbard. Beware of **its naked** edge!"

Then Ospak shook his spear aloft, but the **tall** man stood forth **and** pushed **back his helm and showed the face of Kiartan.**

"Back! **till** I bid you come out," he cried. "My father's sons have sworn to spare no man of you if a single drop of blood is spilt. Back to your hall! We are here to take our due from meadow and barn." Then he let down his helm and returned to the tent, while the Bathstead **men, armed but helpless, sat** silent within, and heard the raiders drive their cattle from the pastures. Bodli was in the high seat, but his face was worn and sad; yet he looked as if he were thinking of gentle things, even while the fierce eyes of Gudrun's brothers scowled upon him. She herself paced restlessly hour after hour through the hall, while old Oswif sat apart with wrinkled brow, unnoticed by the surly warriors.

The sounds of laughter and blowing horns outside became louder and louder, and never ceased till mid-day. It grew more quiet then, though those within still heard the lowing of cattle and the shouts of the victorious drivers.

Then a voice came from the hill-side: "Rejoice, men of Bathstead, that you need hold no autumn feast this year. Come out: we will not harm you now; we have paid ourselves, and all is peaceful."

They did not stir. Then the voice again cried, "What! are you all dead with fear? Come out, I say!"

Then Ospak, with a great oath, cast down his shield and spear and strode out, and the rest followed him, one by one, till Bodli and Gudrun were left alone.

"And you,—will you not go? Do you know who it is that shames us thus?"

"Yes, yes, I know," he said. "Farewell; I will

19*

go, but not without my sword." And he drew his sword, and went among Oswif's sons, who stood foaming and impotent at the door. Kiartan sat in his saddle outside, and his brothers stood around him beside their horses, while a great noise came from the cattle that thronged the way below the hill.

Bodli stepped out and confronted his foster-brother.

"Come, son of Olaf, meet me now," he cried, "for long have I been weary of the earth, and but one thing seems good to me,—that I should take death at your hands."

Then the bright steel shone in the sunlight, and Olaf's sons would soon have ended all, but Kiartan shouted, above the clash of arms,—

"Hold! make a hedge of your shields and thrust him back. It is vain for him to win death. Live, cousin, and get what you may of joy and honor!"

Bodli held back his weapon and retreated into the door-way before the wall of shields. Then Kiartan said,—

"Better, cousin, if you must die by me, that it should be in some noble fight. Yet God grant us many a day before it happens!" Then, turning to the rest, "But listen, you thievish sons of a wise old man. I gave you from Yule till this day to pay your debt. I take it twice told now,

and I leave behind a double shame. This is
my bridal gift. Think well of it."

Bodli still stood in the door-way with drawn
sword, while amid the clang of arms and blare
of horns he saw the herd move up the dusty
road. He saw Kiartan, too, linger behind the
rest and stare at the gray hall whose roof had
so often covered him, and he could fancy that he
sighed as he looked back at its spreading angles.

"Ah, would God I had died by that hand to-
day!" said the hopeless alien; then he sheathed
his sword and was hustled by the sullen and
baffled brothers into the hall.

The time went far differently at Herdholt.
When evening came, Refna, watching from the
knoll, saw a dust-cloud move toward her far
away on the road, and her heart beat fast when
she beheld in its midst helms and spear-heads,
and at last the guarded herd. She bade the
women put on their best array, and placed the
minstrels on either side the path to greet the
band, whose horns by this time blew close to the
garth-gate. Now they passed through the gate
and over the home-field toward the wall, wearing the Bathstead flowers bound upon their
helms, while the cattle were garlanded with
wreaths from their own pastures.

From the close within came joyful cries and
sounds of harp and fiddle, and a shout ran all

along the line of warriors in gay response. Old **Olaf came out** to the door to greet his sons, **and** Kiartan leapt down by Refna's side and threw his arms about her.

"Behold, Refna! the 'Queen's Gift' **is fittingly** paid for," he cried. "These are yours, **sweet, to** put from you all care and every word that grieves you!"

Refna **tried to utter her** thanks, but could find **no** words, and, with a loving cry, hid her face **in** his breast.

"A dear price to pay for a girl's coif!" Olaf **muttered. "W**oe is me that I should live to look **upon these** latter days!"

X.

KIARTAN after this rode fearlessly about the country, and the sons of Oswif made no open attempt to take revenge for his foray into their domain.

But one day, as **three of** the brothers sat together in Bathstead, Ospak came near and said that the gabbling crone Thorhalla had just been to the hall and spoken of Kiartan, whom she saw on the road. She told, too, that Kiartan would **ride to Knoll** in the west, which news she had **learned from** his own lips, for he promised to bring her back half a mark which one owed her **who lived on his way thither.**

"Oh, enough of this gabbling idiot, God strike her blind!" said Thorolf.

"Rather, God keep her eyes, say I," replied Ospak, "for she told me that he would stay three days at Knoll, and then ride through Swinedale home, close by us, and with but few at his back,—two at most. Good luck to his pride! What a chance for us then! Bodli shall lead or die!"

It fell out as the old woman had said, for Kiartan rode from Knoll with goodman Thorkel and twelve others, who brought him well on his way. But where the pass grew wider and opened out into Swinedale, Kiartan stopped his company and said to Thorkel,—

"Thanks to you, goodman, for the guidance; but now get back. I fear nothing between this and Herdholt."

"Well, but there is time enough yet for you to be waylaid before you are safe at home," said the old man. "Let us ride on."

But Kiartan was firm, and bade him and his men farewell, saying that Bodli was still his friend and restrained the brothers, and, besides, he did not ride quite alone, for An the Black and another, named Thorarin, were with him.

Now, early that morning Oswif's sons had taken their stand along a stream, deep in a hollow where the narrow pass turned to the

I.—*p*

south; and there they waited for Kiartan to come by the road. Before he approached, Bodli lay high up on the bank, so that his helm just showed above the dip of the highway, and Ospak went over and accused him roughly of trying to warn his kinsman of the danger.

"Come down," he cried; "we have got you and the cursed Mire-blade in a trap, and we do not mean that you shall escape us."

"If you knew anything of love or honor," said Bodli, "I might tell you why I am here. If I wanted to save Kiartan, I should do it another way. How if I stood beside him?"

"Down with you!" muttered Ospak. "Hold your peace, or he will hear us!"

As Ospak said this they heard the clinking bits of Kiartan's horses, and he came merrily on, singing an old ballad in praise of Odin. Then suddenly the Bathstead horn rang out, and Kiartan drew rein and looked about him.

Instantly the ambushed brothers sprang forth and made toward him. Kiartan and his men leapt down, and he led them toward a rock beside the road, where they stood at bay.

Kiartan looked most noble, as he paused there in shining mail, with his drawn sword ready for the fray; but when his eye fell upon Bodli a change came, and at first he dropped his hands like one who thinks all is over and gives up.

But in an instant his brow cleared, and he hurled his spear at Thorolf, who fell clattering to the ground. "Down goes the thief!" he cried. "Brave men have met more than these and come fairly off."

There was silence then, save for the noise of the mail rings; but now the brothers rushed across the dusty road, there came a confused gleam of swords, and, through the tumult, now and then a sharp cry or groan as the points went home. Yet Bodli stood pale as death beside them with sheathed sword, and raised no hand in the fight.

Presently there was a lull, and the Bathstead men drew off, but the three still held out unhurt, with backs against the rock.

Then Ospak railed at Bodli, and threatened him with shame and hardship if he took home a bloodless sword. But Bodli made no answer. He stood like a man of iron, while the breeze blew his long black hair around his cheek-pieces and fanned his scarlet kirtle.

Then one cried out that they lost time, and they fell to again; but now their strokes were directed most against Thorarin and An. The first of these broke presently from the crowd and ran swiftly away, followed by two stout men from the Bathstead band; but An the Black fell wounded to death, and over him instantly fell

Gudlaug, **Oswif's** nephew, with a **limb** shorn off **by Kiartan.**

Now once again there was a short lull, and then the four fell furiously upon Kiartan, but **soon** gave back; and the noble **son of Olaf, with his** mail-coat rent and **his shield hanging low** down, panted for **breath, but** stood without a **wound.**

Still Bodli was passive; and Ospak, **enraged at his inaction, struck him in the face with** his **blood-smeared hand.**

"**Get home, you half-hearted traitor, and take my blood to Gudrun!**" he **cried.**

Not a word came from Bodli's lips, and his sword rested in its scabbard. **Ospak railed on:**

"**Are you grown too full of dread, O fond lover, to look him in the face** whom you **did not fear to cozen of** his **bride? Why** draw back, when you may now gain **all with one** stroke?"

Then Kiartan, too, called out Bodli's name clear and loud, and at the first sound **Bodli** turned **his face about in a puzzled way, until he caught Kiartan's eyes; then his mouth** quivered and he **hid his face in his mail-clad hands.**

"**They are right,** kinsman, friend of **the old** days, friend well forgiven now," said **Kiartan.** "Come nearer, **that** you **may know my face; then draw** your **sword, and thrust from off the** earth the **fool who has** destroyed your happi-

ness. My life is spoilt. I do not care longer to
bide and vex you, friend. Strike, then, for a
happy life!"

Bodli's hands dropped down, and his face was
full of doubt and shame. Yet he had grasped
his sword even before Kiartan spoke the last
word, and, still trembling, he now drew it forth,
while even the sons of Oswif shuddered at his
wild eyes as he slowly strode toward Kiartan.

The wind moaned on the hill-side, and a far-
off hound barked by some homestead door; but
the dull sound of Bodli's feet and the tinkle of
his mail rings drowned all the other noises as
the space between them lessened.

Like one who looks vainly for help, Kiartan
glanced around, then raised his shield and poised
his sword, as though he meant to fight to the
end. But there came a quivering smile upon
his lips as he gazed into Bodli's dreadful face,
and there was a flash of swords that never met.

"Ah, better to die than live on so!" cried
Kiartan, and his weapons fell clattering to the
road; but almost before they had touched the
bloody ground, Bodli's sword was thrust into
his kinsman's unprotected side. Kiartan fell
down, then, and Bodli flung himself upon the
earth and bent over him and raised his head
upon his knee.

"What have I done? what have I done?" he

20

cried. "I meant to die. 'Twas I who should
have died, not he. Where was the noble sword
I thought to take here in my breast and die for
Gudrun's sake and yours? Oh, friend, do you
not know me? Speak but a word!"

But Kiartan made no answer.

"And will you not forgive?" moaned Bodli.
"Think, brother, of the days I must still endure!"

Kiartan opened his eyes and tried to get upon
his feet, but he failed, and only gazed hard in
Bodli's face.

"Farewell life, farewell Gudrun!" he murmured, then fell back on Bodli's breast and
strove to take his hand, and was dead.

There was a long silence. Presently the
slayer arose and took up his sword. He spoke
now as one having the right to command the
rest :

"Here is a mighty one laid to earth, and yet
it is no famous deed to have done it. His great
heart overcame him, not my sword. Go, all of
you, to Bathstead, and name me everywhere the
slayer of Kiartan. Send hither men to bear the
body to our hall, then let each man of you hide
his head, for you will find it hard to escape
death. I will stay here, but I shall not be
utterly alone."

XI.

WHEN the bearers of Kiartan's bier reached Bathstead, near sunset of that fatal day, a black figure stood in the porch to receive them. The stern face looked cold and gray under its overhanging hood, but about the feet, as if in token that the end of the journey was near, lay the long rays of the dying sunlight.

Every heart in the melancholy throng about Kiartan's body trembled at the thought of meeting Gudrun. She had raved wildly all the long day, and now, when he was borne into the hall where he and she had spent so many happy hours, her grief must overwhelm her and be pitiful to look upon. Could she survive? Could she endure the long grief? These questions were on all lips as the bearers drew near the threshold.

But Gudrun had gained a stern command of herself. She made no outcry, only came near, and in a low voice said, half to them and half to him on the bier,—

"Enter and rest. There is too much change and stir. Rest is good. No one is within but Oswif, and he will not speak. As for me, I am grown tired, and cannot vex you much."

She stepped aside then, and the dark shadows of the porch hid her black dress from view, but the silent throng passed into the dim-lighted hall, afraid to look upon her face.

Bodli went last of all, clashing through the stone porch; but he paused before he had quite passed over the threshold, and, turning slowly around, tried to see her face in the darkness.

"Your will is done," he said. "Are you enough alone, as I am?"

She made no answer.

"I did it for your sake, Gudrun. Speak one word to me before I am crushed to death by my shame."

Then she reached out her hand toward the place where he stood, but did not touch him, and he never knew whether she meant to express her pity or to thrust him farther from her.

Soon the bearers and their followers came trampling slowly out, and Bodli shrank back against the wall to let them pass. When the last one was gone he looked again for her, but he stood quite alone in the dim twilight. He listened yearningly to the noises within, but he did not dare to follow her.

He lingered there, hoping for some favorable sound, till the moon began to shine under the porch eaves; but he heard little, save the faint clink of his own mail as he stirred restlessly about the stone pavement.

"Can she have died with grief?" he wildly

thought. "Oh that she might still say one little word to me who love her so!"

But he peered in vain through the dark reaches of the hall. There was not a sound, not a movement. At last he turned lingeringly away, and his steel war-gear began to sparkle in the open moonlight.

Then there came a loud wail out of the dead hush of the hall, and the house-carles hurried through the gloom with flaring torches.

They came out into the porch, seeking for the cause of the cry; but Bodli knew in his heart that it was Gudrun's cry of despair, and, smitten with a dreadful terror, he fled away into the night.

Bodli came back to Bathstead before the Herd-holt folk removed their fallen kinsman to a grave in his own stead, but he was little loved by any soul of either household, and at last he met death in manly warfare, fighting against his many foes.

Now, after Bodli was slain, and after Oswif had passed away in peace, the dale grew too fearful and full of sad memories for Gudrun longer to remain there, and she exchanged Bathstead for Snorri's hall at Holyfell. There she dwelt with Bodli's grown sons about her, and took to her side one day, in fulfilment of Guest's prophecy, another husband; but he, too, went to the grave before her, and she who had grown blind as she grew in years was again alone for all the long days to come.

But once on a summer evening as Gudrun sat in Holyfell, with another Bodli there beside her, a travelled and mighty man in gay raiment, he, perhaps growing weary of that tranquil life, stirred and sighed heavily.

"Mother," he said, "awhile ago it came into my mind to ask you something. You have loved me well, and this is no great thing to reveal to one who loves you."

She smiled, with her sightless eyes turned on him, but did not answer. Then he went on:

"Which of the men you knew,—who are dead long ago, mother,—which did you love the best?"

Her thin hands pressed one on the other, and her face quivered, as if some memory struggled within her.

"Ah, son! the years go by. When we are young, we call this or that one the worst we can ever know. But yet, as time passes, there comes a day when the old sorrows are fair and sweet to what we must then endure. 'Evil is bettered by the evil that follows it,' says the saw."

They were both silent a little space, then she spoke once more:

"Easy enough to tell about them, son, for my

memory is unbroken. Thorkel was a great chief, bounteous and wise. Bodli, your sire, was mighty ; you would have loved him well. Thord, my husband, was a great man, eminent at the council-board ; and Thorwald,—he was a rash, weak heart, like a stinging weed that must be pulled up. Ah, that was long, long ago."

Bodli smiled.

" You do not speak your true thought, mother. I know these things well."

" Alas, son," she said, " you ask of love. Folly lasts long ; still that word moves my old, worn heart."

She turned till her sightless eyes gazed as though the wall and the hills had melted away, showing her Herdholt in the soft twilight. Then she passionately stretched out her hands as if to embrace all she had lost.

" Oh, son," she wailed " I did the worst to him I loved the most !"

END OF THE FIRST BOOK.

www.ingramcontent.com/pod-product-compliance
Lightning Source LLC
Chambersburg PA
CBHW020558030726
47497CB00007B/1998